Notes on Jackson and His Dead

Hugh Fulham-McQuillan

NOTES ON JACKSON AND HIS DEAD

DALKEY ARCHIVE PRESS

Mclean IL / Dublin

Copyright © 2019 by Hugh Fulham-McQuillan.
First Dalkey Archive edition, 2019.

Library of Congress Cataloging-in-Publication Data
Names: Fulham-McQuillan, Hugh, author.
Title: Notes on Jackson and his dead / Hugh Fulham-McQuillan.
Description: First Dalkey Archive edition. | McLean, IL : Dalkey
Archive Press, 2019.
Identifiers: LCCN 2018026158 | ISBN 9781628972870 (pbk. :
acid-free paper)
Classification: LCC PS3606.U479 A6 2018 | DDC 813/.6--dc23
LC record available at https://lccn.loc.gov/2018026158

www.dalkeyarchive.com
McLean, IL / Dublin

Printed on permanent/durable acid-free paper.

For
my mom, Carmel

In slightly different forms, certain texts in this volume appeared in the following periodicals and online journals: "Spiral Mysterious," "Rigor Terra," "Fog," and "On The Absence of Light" in *gorse*, "Notes on Jackson and His Dead" in *The Stinging Fly*, "Gesualdo" in *Colony*, "Theme on the Character and the Actor" in *Burning Bus*, "Winter Guests" in *Best European Fiction 2018*, and "Skin" in *The Lonely Crowd*.

Contents

That I—this is what I can't say—was terrible: terribly gentle and weak, terribly naked and without decency, a tremor alien to all pretense, altogether pure of me, but of a purity that went to the far end of everything that demanded everything, that revealed and delivered over what was altogether dark, maybe the last I, the one that will astonish death, the one that draws death to itself like the secret that is forbidden it, a piece of flotsam, a still-living footprint, a mouth open in the sand.

Maurice Blanchot, *The Last Man*

It would be an exaggeration to say that ours is a hostile relationship; I live, let myself go on living, so that Borges may contrive his literature, and this literature justifies me. It is no effort for me to confess that he has achieved some valid pages, but those pages cannot save me, perhaps because what is good belongs to no one, not even to him, but rather to the language and to tradition.

Jorge Luis Borges, "Borges and I"

Notes on Jackson and His Dead

IT IS ASTONISHING HOW QUICKLY he fills up a room with all those past selves. When he's been restless, you would believe the Terracotta Army had crossed the sea, stomping along its quiet floor, just to surround him. His wife frequently had to free him from prisons formed from his wake, which, within the past year, had begun to manifest as fully functioning, but lifeless, reproductions, frozen in the position of his last movement: fleshy mannequins in his own image. To save time, and unnecessary worry and terror (which belonged to whom it is difficult to say), Jackson and his wife predetermined exact patterns through their home so that he can move around without creating a dead end. He walks close to the walls of each room, taking narrow tacks into the centre if he needs to get something, say on a table. Yellow strips of tape mark Jackson's optimum paths through their house. I've noticed my assistants have started to follow these without thinking. Even I have, on occasion, felt a relief in following that tape, as if deciding where to place my feet as I walked was a burden generously lifted by those yellow kinesiological lines. I also have a piece, this one blue, attached to my elbow by Jackson's wife, a physiotherapist, to hold my tendons in such a way as to relieve me of pain when I hold the camera.

I never realised how randomly we walk, how inexact and clumsy our primary method of transportation can be. Children and the suspicious know and fight this, but even the most contained of adults will throw their legs forward without a thought beyond a final destination. For a segment of the film—I may

3

use it as an introduction depending on its impact—I replicate Jackson's difficulties by tying a red string to my waist before strolling through a forest. (An assistant ties the other end to the car and holds it taut. Another films me from a distance.) Within minutes my options are narrowed by lines of string looped around the trees. After half an hour I have painted the forest red and stand near the centre in a clearing between two pine trees. About three paces squared. I had previously forbidden my assistants to rescue me until an hour had passed, so I waited, surrounded by my self-imposed, arbitrary restrictions. The footage really makes you think, which is difficult.

Jackson tends to forget his assigned paths when angry or upset. It's fascinating how each mood corresponds to a different pattern of walking. In anger he moves in jagged zigzags, in sadness and rumination his steps take him in ever decreasing circles until he becomes stuck in his centre. Sometimes, and this seems to be dependent on the subject of his ruminations and the speed of his steps, he creates wheels within wheels—jangly spoked bicycle wheels. In happiness he creates great looping patterns that can end anywhere. I took him out to a field where we had a camera placed on a crane. We caught marvellous images of his anger. From high enough, all those dead copies become little dark blotches—you can really understand the pattern of his mind without having to see the grotesque physicality that is its manifestation. There are aspects of cubism there, the geometricity, the distortion—he could be an outsider modernist. I could make him that. With this strange man and his forever-shedding selves as my paint, I could do that.

When he traps himself, after pacing and pacing, usually in the kitchen, until he has no way out, he has to be calm in the midst of them. I don't like their glassy stares that follow you, in that way inanimate things do so eerily, those fresh mannequins with real hair and teeth, so I have my assistants remove him. That's probably why the wife allowed us to film. She used to have to do it and hated it, but now I've allocated someone to take care of all that and she's been able to go back to work. I did it once. When I got through, I wasn't sure which one was him.

It was like finding yourself in a room built of mirrors reflecting somebody else. It was horrible to be crowded by all those things. Jackson has to keep still at that moment. It is imperative he not move so that no more selves form. I had to touch each one to find him. Their skins feels like hardened wax. I found him, warm and pliable, and edged the trolley under his heels, and he shuffled very slowly onto it, and I wheeled him out through his dead past, pushing them aside. It always unnerves me how light they are. They tumble if you hit them from the right angle, especially the unbalanced ones, one foot above the other in the frozen momentum of Jackson's own walk.

It really is a fantastic opportunity to capture movement in all its solid physicality. When we move there is no evidence. If someone was watching you as you stood still, then closed their eyes as you took two steps forward, in the absence of CSI-like instruments they would have only their memory to determine that you hadn't already been standing in your new position; that a movement through space in time had occurred. The observer must trust in their memory. Jackson could never deceive any-one about his movements. His every step is documented by his old flesh. To watch him run is to see an extending diagram of a man running, each position recorded by an exact copy, with him alive at the very end of a line made of his immediate and decaying past. Old or poor recording equipment creates a blur if your subject moves too fast for the shutter. Jackson's selves make that blur physical and real, no longer an artefact of shoddy equipment's attempts to recreate reality. They make that reality true and so make us question what we previously believed—the meaning of truth opened up like an ancient beetle, like an empty shell or flower that is more beautiful to us at night.

Their shelf date is about two days, after that . . . philosophy is dragged from the drawing-room out to the wilderness where it must help those shivering people that surround it. What is death if a man can do it so often and shuffle free each time? Death as a biological imperative, the necessity of which we have yet to dis-cover. He dies to live. I have my assistants truck the dead selves away to the dump after a day, just to be sure. The landfill looks

like the aftermath of something despicable. Note: it might make
a good last scene, an aerial tracking shot revealing mountains
and valleys peopled by his rotting selves: the end at the end, this
is the end, death's dream kingdom, etc.

    We accompany him on his weekly visit to his psychiatrist.
The woman is odd and in my view completely inefficient, as a
professional, and it is very likely, as a human. She propositioned
me once, when Jackson and his wife were settling up with the
secretary. She called me back and said she had always seen herself
as a bohemian but her parents had made her quit painting at a
young age. Then she tried to kiss me. I let her, but up close she
had a sour body odour undisguised by soap or perfume. I pulled
away and said I had to go. I said it quietly, looking deep into her
eyes, the way you relay significant news to someone you care for,
and left her wondering. I didn't mean it to, but the way I said
it left me wondering a little too. Never trust a psychiatrist. She
almost always presents a new pill for Jackson when we sit in her
office. They are side-effect factories housed in pretty antibacterial
cases. None have had any effect on *his* condition. They change
his moods, cause gastrointestinal issues, one even coloured his
skin the shade of ripe tangerines. Seeing him walk down the road
was like watching an orange peel itself in a slow-motion kami-
kaze. It might make for a humorous part of the documentary if
things get a bit heavy. Note: tone.

    Jackson conducted orchestras. He obviously cannot do this
in his current condition—it would be illogical and inefficient
to have more conductors than members of the orchestra. Even
if those conductors are impassive lumps of flesh with only one
movement—hence his fevered visits to specialists of every kind
in search of treatment. I tried to get him to conduct on camera—
the visual impact would be striking—something dramatic and
romantic like Tchaikovsky, even the psychiatrist agreed with me
on that. She is trying more and more to get me to like her since
I refused her—in post-production I will enhance her efforts.
Jackson has become too cowed by events to do anything like
that. He mumbles, something I am told is a new characteristic
of his. He says it would be a nightmare to have his orchestra

see him so out of control. I have watched videos of his perfor-
mances. Even with the sound down you can hear the music in
his gestures, his dripping sweat and ecstasy. He is like a corpse
now, apart from the eyes: all that whirlwind trapped inside
those eyes. The psychiatrist believes conducting may even have
a restorative effect, but he is steadfast; he is made of countless
battalions.

He is cursed with an optimism redolent of an earlier age
and so he doesn't allude to it, but he must be tired of the many
possibilities provided as to what might be causing his troubles.
It seems everyone has had a go, from specialists in physiology to
readers of the future to plain medical doctors. I've interviewed
each one and will enjoy editing their nonsense and bravado. One
of the more unusual, and slightly more plausible, theories as to
what was happening came from a friend of his at the university,
an assistant professor of quantum physics with hair like Medusa,
if her snakes were old and tired of mythology. She suggested that
every time he moved the majority of his body, he was in fact travelling through the multiverse, almost simultaneously inhabiting
each of his infinite selves. She theorised he was the most forceful
of his selves and so they grabbed on to him and landed in this
dimension when he stopped moving. They cannot survive here,
possibly due to the slightly altered content of our air, which may
be toxic to them. They coalesce into the singular and it appears
as if he is shedding a self.

I don't agree with her. Neither does Jackson's wife. She looks
like an older Monica Bellucci and she has a yen for continental
philosophy. If Jackson dies of this, and we all hope he doesn't,
I promise I will look after her every need. Veronica (that's his
wife) thinks his problem is existential. It's to do with a lack of
meaning, she says—in his search for a meaning he is beginning
to disintegrate. If he doesn't find his meaning soon, he will die a
death of fragmentation. This was the first time we had a proper
conversation sans cameras, assistants, Jackson. At first her words
tumbled over those red velvet-cushioned lips like inflexible gym-
nasts, but soon, they stretched and then flipped into the accept-
ing silence I had created as readily as Olympians twisting and

soaring for points: from the perspective of the man in the street
Jackson looks like a perfect specimen, she said. I used to think
he was, especially when I first played cello in his orchestra. I fell
in love with that man. Now that I know him, I see that persona
was about as perfectly put together as his evening wear. Beneath
it he was a collection of shattered mirrors, a broken and poor
imitation of a person. A mirror is not a mirror until it reflects
something, otherwise it's just a piece of glass. (I'm not sure I
understand this, but at the time I was swept along.) You remember when men used to only change their shirt collars and cuffs?
That is Jackson inside. She quoted Kierkegaard at this point (did
I mention how much in love I am?):

As it says in novels, he has now been happily married for several years, a forceful and enterprising man, father, and citizen, even
perhaps an important man. At home in his house his servants refer
to him as "himself." In the city he is one of the worthies. In his
conduct he is a respecter of persons, or of personal appearances,
and he is to all appearances a person. In Christendom he is a
Christian (in exactly the same sense that in paganism he would
be a pagan and in Holland a Hollander), one of the cultured
Christians. The question of immortality has frequently engaged
him, and on more than one occasion he has asked the priest if
there is such a thing, whether one would really recognise one-
self again; which for him must be a particularly pressing matter
seeing that he has no self.

She said it was only natural for a man of Jackson's immense
physicality to present his sickness as a physical thing. He is dying
a slow death and you are recording it for posterity. I interrupted
here to assert my innocence, but she waved my words away as if
she took it for granted that I was observing without helping, that
that was okay. She continued: If he does not find his meaning
he will die. I asked her if she believed in immortality and she
said she did believe but it was of no consequence to the already
living. The self continues, but Jackson needed to find his so that
he could tune into his immortal wavelength. I could see she
wouldn't be swayed from the plight of her strange husband so I
let her talk some more. Then I filmed her walking through an

empty playground holding an impenetrable book of philosophy. European, she said.

Note: instead of one documentary, I could create a series. Formally it would be fitting for a man with so many selves. Financially, it would be beautiful. Even if they decide to end our arrangement before I am ready, I am sure I have enough footage. My assistants film his every moment. They are closer to him as a result (Jackson has not yet spoken to me), they report he enjoys living on camera, that if this thing (he never names it), this multiplicity, kills him, at least he can live out a variety of moments that have yet to be seen. His images will live on in the eyes of his viewers. I've told my assistants to encourage these thoughts of his, at least for now, for if we cannot control the end of Jackson we can control the terms of his continuation. He has recorded messages for Veronica: treatises on music, refutations of her theories, and deeply private communications that made me want to stop watching. Common to each of these is the silence that frequently envelops him. Even in the middle of sentences the words will fall away and Jackson will stare unmoving into the camera for hours at a time, like a man suddenly aware of his existence and all it entails, before resuming his monologue—as if someone had pressed play on a video.

I'm thinking of titles: *The Man Who Carries in Him a Population. Jackson's Search for Meaning. Jackson's End. Jackson and His Dead.* I like that one, it reminds me of *Johnny and the Dead,* which now that I try to remember, I realise I cannot remember what it is about. Note: have assistants look up *Johnny and the Dead* before using *Jackson and His Dead* as a title.

Spiral Mysterious

VIDEO 1. BLACK LEATHER-GLOVED hands caress a variety of knives on a red velour-covered surface; music, languorous and discordant, distorted bells and piano keys like heavy footsteps; women's sighs curl through chords; a house is seen from the outside, through shaking leaves, at night; floor-to-ceiling windows frame a woman lying on a white couch inside; she is poised; we are closer, almost pressed against the window; she is reading a book; we are so close the title can be read on the upper left of the page: *New Notes on Edgar Poe*; now we are behind her, reading the words of the upper paragraphs until they are obscured by her sleek dark hair; we are watching a gloved hand clutch a short dagger with gold-embossed wings above its handle; the dagger falls and stabs, repeatedly, in an arc over her head and into her chest; the book falls to the floor closing itself; we see her dead eyes; the video ends with a black screen.

This video is clean, and confident in its style. It is aware of potential missteps. It is a murder, of course, but a stylised one, not that that excuses the happening in the final scene, but it cannot be denied that this style lends a certain sympathy toward the author.

Video 2. There is a jarring absence of music; black leather-gloved hands slowly twist a blade in the darkness, reflecting a glint of light toward the camera; there is a barely audible sound—a triumphant gleam redolent of cartoons; a gloved hand carries the knife, angled downward, past a banister; heavy breathing; a woman slumps on a couch reading a brightly coloured magazine, holding a purple mug that steams in the short light of her reading lamp; the rest of the room is darkened yet bright, as if the moon had bored through the ceiling; she looks up; we approach from her side; "Is that you, Barry?" There is no reply. She shakes her head, "Must be this bloody house settling." She turns the page; the camera jumps and we see the pores of her nose, the granules of mascara clumping her eyelashes; the mug falls to the floor; the camera zooms out some feet in front of her; "I know you," she says, her voice quivering; there is no reply, but we, the camera, the viewer, the almost-killer move toward her as one; "What . . . what are you doing with that knife?"; we, it, they do not reply; the camera jumps again and we see the broken mug, its shards dripping tea, her nerveless hand propped clumsily against the floor; contributors' credits roll over her dead body. A theme tune plays.

Awful. Artless: this second video could not be more unaware. And to think, this is a so-called professional production. The culmination of an Irish soap opera. Were they asleep when they shot this scene?

I should explain. Video 1 is a recording of a possible murder. Video 2 is a scene from a popular Irish soap opera depicting a murder. The actor who played the killer in this latter video, in the soap opera, was found comatose in his apartment having been attacked by someone as yet unidentified. This attack seems to have occurred on the day Video 1 was sent to our department, and simultaneously released on the internet, on the same day the soap opera's scene aired.

I had questions for the actor. I have asked these as I sat beside his hospital bed, watching distant wards through the windows, watching nurses smoke cigarettes in empty rooms, exhaling through the open windows that look out to the concrete square below. The smoke is swept up and briefly shapes the wind. My questions are absorbed into his ears, his skin. I don't know if he heard—if they reverberated around his sleeping mind—or if they sunk inside him without his knowing. I have thought about those video endings, how apt that they finish with a death, as if the videos were living things reincarnated every time we press play, dying when they end.

The scene from the soap was broadcast on television, then pulled on account of our investigation. It is probably back in rotation by now, playing on Sunday mornings, watched, studied by morbid teenagers on YouTube, by researchers, by fans.

The email sent to the station, which linked to the video of the murder, provided directions to a large house, hidden from the road by extensive gardens, on an iconic Dublin street. The owners, a young and attractive couple, expressed mild confusion on our arrival. Their clear faces betrayed an absence of shock at the possibility of someone having been murdered in their home. I have come to accept, to expect this reaction. I recognised their living room as the scene of the videoed crime. I examined the leather sofa where the girl's murder was recorded. A team trawled the room with their delicate equipment, viewing the marble tiles, cream rug and leather sofa in atomic detail, yet they could find no evidence of a break-in. There was no body. No blood. No book. When my questions began to lose form and direction, in desperation, I asked them about the book. The owners said they preferred documentaries, and asked who Poe was. They sat me down and offered coffee and almond biscuits when my dizziness came on. They apologised when they could not identify the girl from the video still I showed them. The woman was helpful, but not suspiciously so. I studied her mannerisms and features but found nothing in them to relate to the girl. The man busied himself foaming milk, grinding beans, running a noisy coffee machine. When he finally finished the task, his focus fell to his phone. The woman excused his behaviour by explaining he was expecting an important call, one that might change their lives. I left when the phone rang.

The central premise of our investigation was the comparison of the two videos, with the belief that by examining the similarities between them, we might be able to decipher their shared language, and by doing so, identify the creator of the first video: the murderer. It would have been a useful exercise if the two videos had had many similarities, but the only shared aspects of the videos are that both attempt to immerse the viewer in the events through the use of first-person camera positions, and both tell the cut-down story of a murder. In terms of style . . . Style is voice, voice is identity.

Soon after I had begun my analysis, an activity I knew could only result in failure, something happened to me. At the time, I barely realised it. I have never felt comfortable with cultural norms. Films strike me as childish things, as does television. I guess I enjoy art galleries. (I like the search for understanding, for meaning in each frame in those unending rooms. The knowledge that I will never know why the artist used that perspective, seemed to swipe at the canvas just there, the acceptance of never knowing. And the colours, too.) This quiet pursuit was a poor preparation for what had become, in my absence, acceptable entertainment. The scenes I witnessed during my work were almost never meant to be the end product (and when they were, the director was usually wired violently differently to the majority). Crime scenes were the detritus of crime, the fingerprints of criminals. They weren't meant to be enjoyed with a bag of popcorn, a cup of tea.

By witnessing these videos, produced with the aim of immersing the viewer in the recorded crime, real or fictional, I was infected by a guilt that did not belong to me. I had been burdened by the guilt of someone who would perform such acts, not the complete guilt—I still clung to reality's edge—but not a complete lack of it either; my guilt balanced on a scale that tipped toward the mysterious emotional state of one who murders. Recording such a singular act insured it would be viewed, and by insuring it would be viewed, the person, or persons, knew the guilt would be shared, that the burden would be divvied out among the creator and the audience. It didn't matter whether a crime had occurred or not, what mattered was its presentation as entertainment. This is what that soap opera aspired to: to grit, to an insidious tourism of the dark-infested parts of life and the shadow-eaten souls that live there; to place the viewer there, like chucking a rabbit down a coal mine, as if to see what it would look like when covered in dirt. This is supposed to be entertainment.

I realise I am forced to use a language that fails to distinguish between fiction and reality in describing these videos. Yes, one was real, but the other was not false, not fake and not false—a pretence. A pretence cannot be distinguished from the real unless it is signposted, by amateurism or professionalism, or some other definable boundary. But when the real is dressed in the clothes of art, and when the fiction comes clothed in what you would expect from the real—the chaotic, swirling real—how are you supposed to react? How are you supposed to react when the act of murder is presented as entertainment? What is the viewer supposed to do with that, unless it is meant as a preparation for the possibility of this occurring in your own life; I cannot believe a soap opera would have such a noble intention. There had been a deliberate blurring of the divide between fiction and reality, and through my repetitive viewing of the videos, I had been forced to choose between producing an immunity to it or letting it crawl inside my heart like a black, living root.

My superior said there were rumours circulating—wholly independent of any one person as rumours so often appear to be, ghostly, shadowy whispers that seep from the walls if you are to believe the originator—suggesting I had lost the plot, that I lost it a long time ago. He didn't ask me if I had lost it, just put the idea in my head, let it swirl around, and once he put it in there, I was helpless to do anything but ruminate on the possibility of everyone else being right and my being opposed to them because I had indeed become lost. To return my thoughts to some kind of plot, to create a plot that I could hold on to, in the absence of any real evidence, I knew I had to turn away from my video analysis.

From the start, my colleagues believed the videos were more than connected by their supposed similarities, that they were two components of the one sequence. It was assumed the actor enjoyed the sensations of murder in his initial soap opera scene so much that he wanted to try it for real. And lacking the boundaries of decency, respect, ethics, fear, behind which most of us live, he was free to recreate his actions in the real.

Details taken from interviews with the soap opera's crew formed the basis of my colleagues' consensus. During the filming of the pivotal scene, the actor is reported to have insisted on numerous repetitions. He also insisted on making contact with the female actress's clavicle with his rubber knife—despite this not being required, as the camera veers respectably away at the point of contact. (I have decided this is about the only thing respectable about the camera, about every camera held by every cameraman in the history of photography.) According to the director, the actor cited as his reasoning the importance of revealing life's truths in his art. Interviews taken with those on the set that day relay a feeling of unease at this actor's incessant need for a realism that most preferred to consume within the safety of their own entertainment.

Perhaps the actor was unhappy with the final take, and when viewing it that night, as he ate his evening meal, felt disappointed with his performance. So our actor decided to produce his own take, with real "stakes," as my colleagues hilariously, and repeatedly, stated. That was the creeping understanding of my colleagues.

Even if I were to follow in their plodding mental footsteps, I would find it necessary to veer off the path at the point of their reasoning for the actor's, supposed, retake. The stylistic differences between the two videos are too great to ignore, but that is exactly what my colleagues had done and continued to do despite my report on this point.

Style, I have come to believe, is everything.

For one thing, the first video has music that is fitting to the mood and atmosphere. In the second video there is none; in its place are a series of jarring sounds, the clumsily enhanced breath of the killer, the laughable dialogue, the sound effects of the knife's stabs which you can almost picture taking place in the local butcher's shop, microphone held to the belly of pork repeatedly stabbed while customers wait for their sausages and rashers. Clumsy. The production, direction, scenery, acting, of the second video, the supposedly professional video, is clumsy. If I were the actor forced to work in such surroundings, I would almost understand his need to produce something aesthetic, something that strains toward beauty no matter how heart-rending and despicable its subject matter. Who could work in the environment of a soap opera?

In the silence—which I find so difficult these days—I turned the question on myself: Who could work in a job like this? I refused to answer, and instead, immersed myself in thoughts of the videos. This soon led to my viewing those two scenes. I had them on a loop on two screens, playing over and over. They had become a sort of home to me. As I analysed them for clues, for similarities that I knew I would never find unless I created them myself. As I watched, I saw my reflection in the screen, my face tight with anticipation. It built in me, independent of my rational thoughts. I watched again and again, and every time that anticipation would wind and wind until the end of the scene, until the murder was complete; and at the climax—when a line had been newly drawn between the living and the dead—I would feel an overpowering sense of relief that, yes, allowed me to sleep. I felt guilt creep through me then, seeking the empty cavities of my sinuses, the hollows of my joints, the spaces in between my organs. What I was feeling may have been even greater than what the killer felt. To record the act requires preparation, practise, spending hours perfecting the rainbow arc of the knife into the chest while capturing everything necessary within the frame of the camera that stands in for the fleshy surrounds of the eye. (With practice anything can take on the dullness of boredom.) The actor from the first video could not have held the camera so still while exerting such passionate stabs. It became clear to me that he must have had an accomplice, someone to hold the camera. I watched the video again, and marvelled at its framing. This wasn't a tourist, or amateur enthusiast, this was someone who lived for capturing the perfect scene within the frame of the screen. This was an artist. I would have preferred to have discovered something different at that point, something more illuminating, but it was the best I could do, which I think was understandable considering my situation.

Lacking leads and bodies, the investigation soon fell apart. My colleagues found warmer corpses, they dismissed the video as a prank, dismissed the actor's attack and subsequent coma as a cold case not yet cooled. I was about the only one left in the department who needed a solution. I revisited the house from the video. The woman was home, but she was busy with work, something about a radio documentary she was starring in. I had the downstairs to myself and spent some time tracing the protagonist's footsteps through the garden, noting the areas where an assailant might gain entry. When I emerged from the bushes at the end wall, I saw the woman, through an upstairs window, sitting at a desk or table with her head in her hands. She appeared to be naked. I watched her for a moment, then walked through the patio doors and followed that recorded path, which I knew so well, directly to the side of the couch, and practised the swing of the knife as it stabbed the young woman from the video. As I followed the downward trail of my imaginary weapon, I noticed two dark patches on the cream carpet by the couch. Dark like two dried blood drops. I continued to swing my knife, and watched as the blood crept down her arm, along her hand, dripping from her index and middle finger onto that rug. Drying over hours, or was it days?

The initial inspection had recorded nothing useful, not even errant hairs. Everything had been as clean as you would expect from a well-kept home in that part of the city. I took a photo with my phone before calling her down. There was no reply. I went upstairs calling her name, gun in hand. She was nowhere. I went outside to the garden again. Her bedroom window was obscured by steam and I could not see. I left a note with my contact details by the phone.

I continued to visit the hospital, almost daily, to sit beside the sleeping actor. The answer was inside him. I got to know the nurses who checked on his beeping machinery; some were friendly, others operated as if I wasn't there. In lieu of questioning my half-dead suspect, I directed questions toward myself, for what exact purpose I don't know; it had become a habit of mine during the investigation. The nurses in distant wards still sent their smoke spirals into the wind and I still watched from that quiet room.

According to the on-set interviews, the actor had been working on the programme for five years. Initially his character was meant to be the comic relief, "an idiotic man-child who failed in everything he tried, yet never lost his 'joy' de vivre" (screenwriter—Jeff). Before his first year was over, the screenwriters found this role was a poor fit for our actor. Previously, he had struggled to live off of random stage plays, frequently appearing in pantomimes, and when drunk (which was a frequent occurrence) he often stated he would have made a perfect Duncan. He had trained in London with RADA. The screenwriters soon incorporated aspects of his personality into his character. Apparently this is done to ease the need to actually act, something that can hinder a production according to the producer of the programme. "You can't control all the variables, but seen as the actors are the most volatile you gotta make their job as easy as possible" (producer—Gary). I rang this producer to find out more about the actor.

Gary told me that most soap opera characters are a combination of the screenwriters' need to create interesting plotlines and the characteristics of the actors themselves. The line between the actor and the character frequently became confused. Travellers played travellers, sociable actors became sociable characters. He laughingly recalled an old actress who had played a post office mistress in the programme. After she was fired at the age of seventy-five, she was hired as the post office mistress in her local post office. It was reported in the national newspapers. The government even placed a plaque outside the office commemorating her role in the programme, and in the nation's heart. She changed her name by deed poll to her character's name. She stalked the actors who had been part of her on-screen family, refusing to call them by anything but their on-screen names. They filed for restraining orders against her. She repeatedly broke these and spent time in prison. Each time she was released she was found on the set or at the gates to the studio begging to be let in. I'm not sure what happened to her because Gary couldn't stop laughing. I had to hang up. I distinctly remember feeling ill after our talk and having to lie down with the curtains closed. The room seemed to vibrate.

They made the actor the resident toff, a snob with a mysterious past. Soon he became a suspect in a murder case. It had become a tradition for the entire year's plot lines to build up to a gory moment on Christmas day when someone in the show would kill, or die in a road traffic accident. He was going to be the star of that year's storyline. One actress baulked at the identification of the actor with his latter role. She said the actor was a serious man, but he wasn't dangerous. "He had high ideals" (Susan—actress). Another actress said Susan had "designs on him" (Janice). Most of the cast's statements relayed similar attitudes, professing his high-mindedness and innate goodness, yet the technical workers suggested he was prone to moods and had a violent temper. Gary refuted their claims: "They're only actors, mate!" I presented a report detailing as much of the above series of events as related to the case—free of digressions, unnecessary thoughts, and dead ends—to my supervisor: the bare facts.

Weeks passed. I missed a call from the lady of the house from the video. I remember the message: "I know who the killer is, the girl, too. I found something that explains everything. I'm going to stay in a friend's house. You can call me on—" The answering machine cut her off at that point. I had been listening to the message when my supervisor appeared in the doorway beckoning me to his office. He told me to give it up. To stop looking for something that wasn't there, that I was being played. When I insisted, he said, "There are some things we can never know. This is one of them." The case was closed. The actor's attack was designated as something separate, something for someone else to worry about. I couldn't let that happen and he knew it.

I have been trained to find answers. I came to that job because of my need to know, to understand. I have never been satisfied with what I have found, and yet, I have continued to seek. Looking back over my life, answers, especially those that lie waiting at the end of the most difficult of questions, have never been worthy of the search. It was always when I was mired in the unknown and mysterious that I have felt most alive. The answers were the clean-up at the end of the party, but I placed more importance on finding them than anything else. When I found an answer, I immediately sought another so that I could experience that ambiguity once more. It was an addiction. I realise that now.

My superior may have been trying to tell me this, to be content with the journey, or he may not, but that is what resonated with me. He may have said more, but time has condensed his words. Be content with the journey, I remember him saying. I have found this wisdom repeated in some very good self-help books since. It has shown me how to come to terms with the story of me, of my understanding of things, of violence, of how I relate to the world.

This is what I know:

The murder scene becomes a murder scene only when the murder is complete, otherwise it is simply a scene of violence, a violence that becomes more extravagant the closer it crawls toward the annihilation of the person it is being done unto, until they are no longer a person but evidence of having once been. This is what I understand now. In viewing the scene of murder, there is an anticipation of the end. At the first insight that this violence, this drama will continue until death, a tension tightens inside the audience members until the the death is done, at which point their collective shoulders drop and they sigh and congratulate themselves on seeing it through, when really, they wanted it to happen, they silently, or not so silently, cheered on the total and vast and cosmic annihilation of a person, imagined or not, a representation of a member of our species. Considering the amount of time we have lived on this planet, every scene of every murder acted, written, and painted on screen or canvas for our entertainment must have previously been performed with the sole aim of bringing about the end of some mother's child. Every murder as entertainment is a repeat of something that deserves more respect than the screen, than the pages of piece-meal joined together by a plot and words, can and will allow. What is the use of my even thinking these thoughts if not to luxuriate in them, to wash in the blood of others. All possible murders have already occurred.

The guilt which had grown so great within me as to become an inner layer hidden somewhere between my skin and my memories, this guilt, I realised, was borne not of the first-person view of these two scenes, not of all the killings I have witnessed in my life, but of my desire to witness the fulfilment of the murder in each of the videos, whether they were real or a pretence, it didn't matter anymore. The resolution was what I desired. The tyranny of resolution binds me to these deaths even now, fifteen years after these events took place. I cannot stop writing about this. I have written pages and pages, filled bins with pages, dumped fat black sacks of them on empty roadsides, I am forever editing until I have found that which I need to say. I will never find that. I cannot find it. Resolution is murder. There can only be one end, and we should not be able to choose when and where that occurs, and we should be content with that.

I remember visiting the house one last time. The blood drops had been cleaned. The couple were excitable, jittery. They gave me so much attention that I felt a relief on leaving their home; a dense atmosphere had crept into its rooms. They were on the verge of telling me things that would not have been good for me to hear. The actor's coma continues and I still sit with him. I still watch those nurses sneaking cigarettes in desolate rooms, still watch their smoke spiral when they exhale through open windows.

The Art of Photography

I WANT TO SPEAK NOW about the theatre bar. I sat in a chair by the window. Outside, the car park was full, and mostly dark. I stood by the wall, leaning my elbow on a shelf where I placed my glass. Above the shelf hung a black-and-white photograph of a man in rags: a theatrical image. When that image was captured, there might have been a crowd of people sitting in chairs in a dark room in front of him, or there might only have been the photographer. In looking at him—I was looking quite intently—I became photographer, audience, darkness; and judge: I did not like his posture.

From where I stood in the theatre bar I could hear the dramatic speaking and spurted clapping of the show but not enough to make sense of it. I had arrived late and was not allowed in. My drink was thus complimentary. More photographs hung in apparent disorganisation across the walls. Whenever I see a jumble of such on a wall that is not a charity shop or squat I get a headache—like my head is being squeezed by a thick, and manicured, pair of hands—my head aches thinking about the measurement and precision required to make it look haphazard yet pleasurable, to present an illusion of disorder while retaining such order. All the photos were black and white. All the persons were still and trapped in their pretence, hung in a perfectly organised web of same. And where was the organiser? Missing, and with a web so full of meaty fiction all stuck to those walls—or had that individual also succumbed? Out of necessity, and a certain duty, I inherited that web. I became the spider.

I asked the barman, as he poured drinks in readiness for the patrons, if he were an actor, if he had ever acted. I had been silent for a long time so when I spoke my voice remained within my mouth. I asked again. He told me most people working in the theatre building are actors of some sort. He snarled, like a dog, and I saw he had a gold filling. I wasn't sure if this was an act or something more authentic. I sat on a barstool, though not too close to him. Very good, I said. The audience clapped again. He smiled and said, "They'll be here soon enough. Keep an eye on yourself once they get in, else you'll lose—" A plastic glass fell and spilled its red liquid across the bar. It crossed the polished wood, following those grains so like dried riverbeds, and began to drip down to the beige carpet. I left for the bathroom.

When I closed the bathroom door behind me and stepped back into the main corridor I am sure I was about to leave the building. Why wouldn't I? The corridor was empty of patrons, and lined with even more monochrome photographs of people I could never recognise: each standing on what were obviously stages, with obviously false backdrops; there was one with a painted apple tree, as if the audience were supposed to believe that was a real, growing organism! I knocked that one off the wall and whispered the saying about a tree falling in the forest and nobody hearing; and I put great vehemence into those words.

Those words opened themselves against me, unfolding their trees until they stood irregularly, filling the corridor, their branches spreading and the walls naturally spreading until I stood before them, still and mostly silent, and the carpet was covered by the dead of the trees—their broken branches and forgotten leaves. The forest lumbered and creaked and suspecting it of falling on my poor body, suspecting it of making an example of me, because trees do not have ears and so nobody would hear, I retreated four steps. It followed: advancing in haphazard formation, shorn and sharpened limbs trained on my torso by that prancing and vicious avant-garde. I froze, eyes closed.

When I opened them the corridor was empty: just me and the photographs and that bare space on the wall where the photo had hung: a clean rectangle edged by dirt, made by it. This made me uncomfortable. I decided I would return home, or go to another place, one with more people in it, one far from this building with its marching forests, but instead I turned left and followed those trees the short distance back to the bar. Curiosity led me, I think. The windows were steamed up and I had to wipe a hole with my sleeve to see the car park was just where it was the last time I looked. This was a relief.

The bar itself had elaborate carvings along its outer wall, just where patrons' knees would rub against as they perched on their stools. The carvings resembled figures of the tarot, at least what I know of it. There was a man hanging by his foot in the one closest to me, and beside it I recognised the Belladonna of the rocks who, incidentally, seemed to tower over the body of the barman who lay on the floor. Initially I assumed that the red on his white shirt was that wine which he had so inadequately wiped at, but no, it was blood. Served him right. The ceiling looked damp then, darker than before.

I took a photo of him (with flash). One of his full laying out, and then—standing over his body so as to remove it from the frame—one of his face. I took a photo of him with the carved bar in the background. Then, standing on the bar, beside the trickling wine, I took another. I leaned over the bar and stretched my phone down so that I captured the window in the back-ground. His blood was seeping into the beige carpet, mixing with the dripping wine. The audience clapped and I heard some idiot shout BRAVO! BRAVO!

I stepped back into the corridor and, keeping clear of the photographed images, and of course, the fallen one (which, inci-dentally had cracked its own glass), went down to the box office. Through the opening I could see a teenager looking at his phone. "Excuse me," I said, "but could I possibly use your printer real quick?" I stood there in my tuxedo, smoothing my very white shirt front as I spoke. The teenager was wearing jeans and a woollen jumper and said sure. He lingered beside me as I stood by the printer. I said, "Do you mind?" And I cleared my throat before I said this, thinking I could just as easily knock him out there with nobody around to know.

I printed the five of my photos: seven copies of each, all in black and white. On returning to the bar, I unhooked that first photo of that actor—bent forward, theatrical rags—from the wall and removed the actor from the frame. That monstrosity of a posture, born of mirror gazing. One should not pretend suffering, of all things, not that. I lowered the corner of his photo into a candle on the shelf. I kept lowering it until the candle flame caught on and it all happened very quickly and I stamped out what was left of it. I laid out my photos of my barman scene and chose one with the misted window as background to replace that morally ragged actor. My photo looked perfect on the wall. You could just see where I wiped a hole in the window. The mist became an inner frame through which the darkness of the outside could be seen. Now that was truth.

I removed the next photo, and replaced it with my close-up of the barman's serious face. I continued in this manner until I had run out of prints; by then I had replaced every photo in the bar. Some of the frames were the wrong size—too small for my photos—but I just folded the images so that some would only show the legs of the carved Belladonna, or a rectangle of carpet with the stain creeping in from the corner. When the audience wasn't clapping, and the actors weren't shouting in their theatrical manner in that other room forbidden to me, the wine dripped onto the worn leather of the bar stool, reminding me of those times I have walked outside after a wild storm and heard the rain dripping from an overwhelmed leaf onto the ground where that single dripping sounded so strange so immediately after the maelstrom, as if nature were suddenly and sullenly apologising for the destruction it had wrought. Thinking about all that liquid made me quite thirsty and I helped myself to more wine. I sat again in my seat by the window, and again wiped at the glass because it had again misted over. The car park had disappeared, just as I initially suspected it might. I resigned myself to wait for the interval.

I very quickly bored of this and returned to the box office down the corridor. I cleared my throat, and once the teenager had looked up, said, "I'm awfully sorry, but would you mind

if I used the printer one last time, it's an emergency you see."
I flashed my teeth. The teenager was much quicker in obliging
this time and I printed out the same number of photos and
walked back up to the bar. It was hot; I loosened my bow-tie
with a finger.

When I had been standing by the printer, I had been thinking about my work—it had pleased me and I had felt content,
but seeing it on my return, I felt ashamed: How could I have felt
good? It was clearly unfinished. Crying for completion, reaching
out from those black frames for my hands to become its hands.
The barman was lying exactly the way he had lain before. I
had another glass (this time I am sure I chose the white), then
covered his face with my photo of his close-up. Continuing in
this way, carefully tearing the photos with a little green plastic
sword from behind the bar, I covered each part of his body
with my photographical representations. This was tiring and
I drank many plastic glasses of wine while I worked. When he
was completely covered by my images of himself, I replicated the
viewpoints of my original photos so that I wasn't really photo-
graphing him but my representation of him. I had removed the
barman from my photos while retaining his image. It felt very
philosophical and right, but most importantly, it felt natural.

I returned to the box office. It was thankfully empty (I was
sure I would have knocked out that frail, self-righteous teenager
if I saw him again). I printed double the previous amount of my
new photos and took them back to the bar. I remained happy
with what I saw, there was an overwhelming sense of justness,
or justice—both, I think. I took my remaining photos into the
hall and considered using them to replace each of the photos of
those pretenders that hung along the walls, but then the teenager
appeared in the corridor, walking in my direction, and the look
he gave me! He stopped by a set of double doors, sighed, took a
deep breath, and opened them with a flourish. I then heard the
clapping, or I heard that there had been clapping all that time
and that now there was only a dripping sound and people were
filling the corridor and someone must have bumped into me,
a lot of them bumped into me, spilling my photos all over the

carpet. "Please," I said, "do you mind?" I said (using *that* tone), and they continued and I was being carried along backward into the bar and we all gathered together in what was really a small room and the teenager was there behind the bar pouring drinks quite fast.

I stood by myself. I found a spare bit of space and stood there by the shelf where I had first stood that evening with my complimentary drink. That was gone, which I thought strange. There was a ring mark where I had placed it on the wood but the glass had disappeared—I examined the wood, ran my finger over its barely secret trails, just in case.

Some of the patrons, those who were also alone, and who had not yet become part of a conversation, they looked at my photos and I felt like a parent almost, a parent whose children finally stand upon a stage and everyone clapping and me shouting BRAVO! BRAVO! Because it's fine when it's your own children, it's obligatory I would have thought. Those patrons looked like they were in an art gallery—they were contemplating my art, and I suddenly had the awful thought that they might only be pretending to look at the photos and really were feeling anxious about having nobody to talk to, and were inwardly cringing at the noise and seeming nonsense of those conversations closest to them.

"I think I recognise him," I heard one solitary woman say to another solitary man. "Yes," he said, "me too, wait, I know this, wasn't he in . . ." So they were paying attention to my work, very good, very good, I thought, serves him right, I thought. The two were no longer solitary and I became slightly envious, as you do on these occasions. They moved slightly to the left to another of my works. I followed. Two short steps. "And what about him, I'll give you three guesses," she said, and she winked. "Uh-oh, I didn't study for this," he said. She laughed despite his complete lack of humour: his response was utterly unfunny, I am not lying. So they were making a game of my photos, okay, I thought, that's fine—but it's not. He guessed and she didn't seem to care about what he said, but his eyes, his lips, they were of the utmost importance to this woman. I knew what was happening.

They moved to the next photo, one in which I artfully show only the misted glass of the window. "Ah, I know this one," he said, without her prompting. "No you don't," I said, but I hadn't spoken in a while and my voice was a whisper quickly swallowed by the conversing babble. I strode toward them, first pushing aside an elderly man, then what appeared to be a child but actually was a short woman with a pageboy haircut wearing purple dungarees. Before I reached them I heard the girl say, "Of course you do, she was in the show tonight!" But she wasn't, it wasn't, they were looking at a photo of a misted window! I stood beside them now and they turned to look at me. "What's your game?" I said. They began to explain how they were guessing where they had seen each actor before, I interrupted: "These are my photos of the barman and this bar, the room you are standing in, he died you know." They stared at me blankly. I raced to the window and wiped at the condensation. The car park was still missing. It was black outside. I ran down to the box office, pushing at the people in my way, who all seemed very steady, so that I ended up shuffling for minutes at a time until I reached the door to the outside after what must have been half an hour. It was black outside. I tried to leave but even the pavement was missing. My foot shot through the darkness and I would have fallen through myself if I hadn't caught a hold of the door handle. Suddenly everything went black, then I opened my eyes and saw it was only the street and sky that were black, or gone, empty? and the noise seemed black, too, there was a hollow sort of silence, like an echo of silence out there. Steadying myself I returned to the bar. The patrons had thankfully returned to the show. It was quiet again, apart from the dripping wine, and the sporadic applause escaping through those double doors. I was very afraid of what it was behind those doors. Theatres can be bloody places, I thought. People wear ugly, green gowns and stain your skin with iodine; all sorts go on in there. This clapping, how painful it must be. And all that shouting! I gathered my photos, which had been horribly trampled, from the floor of the corridor and hurried away.

In the bar I sat in my seat by the window and, after pouring the remains of the bottle all over myself, plastered the photos to my body so that the photos of the photos of the reddened shirt front of the barman lay on top of my white shirt front, and tuxedo jacket. It was lucky that I had my photos all printed because the body of the barman was gone. Dragged inside the theatre's secret heart, I bet. He was an actor, he said, and surgeons operate in such places, I knew. He was an actor so I'd make him act through my photos. "Pretend all you like, you're dead," I said. Must have got caught up in the crowd. Taken inside the darkness at the centre of the theatre. I was about to cover my legs in my photos of his legs but this was difficult to do when sitting so I lay down on the carpet which had been stained by so much spilled wine and that little bloodletting. When I was happy that my legs were covered I did the same to my arms, then my face, and especially my ears. My body remained my body and became another body, and a stage. I waited then, for the teenager so he could take the photos of me—and the patrons, of course, for them to see. In time, I thought, I would show them our death.

Gesualdo

The enclosed pages were folded inside a rare copy of Gesualdo da Venosa's biography, which I was fortunate to find in an Edinburgh bookshop. A name and address were inscribed on the front page. I hope you don't mind, but I could not help reading through this fascinating account . . . did you write it? I myself am something of a writer and I suspect our interest in Gesualdo is of a similar nature. I look forward to hearing from you.

Yours faithfully,
Edward

By the laws of classical physics, Carlo Gesualdo should remain dead. Fortunately I cannot think of a law, including those of the natural sciences, that has not been violated. I pry two analgesics from their stubborn foil and swallow with a glass of water. As I massage my throat, my fingers are drawn to the edges of the gauze that covers my face. I pull away from the urge to reveal what is hidden, and begin.

To speak of myself, I must first speak of others, how else can one know of one's self if not by reference to another? When one has been alone for a long time, the world tends to creep toward the skin, filling in the gaps and the creases, until one finds that one has become the world. There are times, however, when this occurs between people, when the world retreats, as skin covers skin and thought flows in between. The following perfectly illustrates the mysterious ways in which the labyrinths of our lives can join with one another until it is difficult to know which corridor leads to whom and from where that distant coughing comes.

In the final pages of his diary, written shortly before his stroke, Charles Baudelaire instructed himself to "Pray every morning to God, the source of all power and all justice . . ." If I were to end the quote here it would be understandable, it would reach out from the page and pull from the reader a sliver of empathy or meet them in the middle distance to produce a foreshadowing of their own mortality with its inevitable questions. There is more, the full line reads "Pray every morning to God, the source of all power and all justice, and to Poe."

The stroke, which arrived less than seventy-two hours after he had written these words, affected the left hemisphere of his brain, thus paralysing the right side of his face, and his right arm. I read that he developed a lesion, a disruption in the neural paths between the, intriguingly named, Broca's and Wernicke's areas, resulting in what is termed global aphasia. I must, for a moment, marvel at the idea of a part of the brain being named after a person, as if the brain were territory uncharted, a vast landscape without life, and it might be for the little that is known of it, and the all that remains outside of our knowledge (and within such easy reach). The stroke ruptured the paths between these two conquered areas, leaving Baudelaire without his precious words.

After a lifetime of writing poetry that would secure his place among French literary immortals such as Rimbaud, Verlaine, and Mallarmé, he was now reduced to the use of one phrase: "*Cré nom!*" When asked if he was hungry, he damned God, when asked if he would receive guests, if he would like some air, if he was ready for his evening meal, he could only damn God for the fate that had robbed him of his ability. He damned God, but not his literary idol, his intercessor, Edgar Allan Poe.

Baudelaire's obsession with the American poet began at a young age. He learnt English so he could read his poetry unencumbered by careless translators. He was the first to translate all of Poe's works, taking solace from the details of his biography, as I have done with Gesualdo (and the other). Poe became an ideal to Baudelaire, who, in turn, strove to become a mirrored image of his hero. I quote a letter in which Baudelaire recounts his earliest memories of reading Poe's work:

I found . . . believe it or not, poems and tales which I myself had vaguely thought of writing, and which Poe had been able to work out to perfection.

Reading these lines launched shivers of recognition, leaping from vertebra to vertebra, down my spine. Separated by a number of years, a passage from a later letter tells the story of a man who, through his obsessive study, has discovered—or by the sheer force of will, developed—a supernatural connection between himself and another. Baudelaire wrote:

The first time I opened one of his books, I saw, with terror and delight, not only subjects I had dreamed of, but sentences I had conceived, which were written by him twenty years before . . .

If this were not exciting enough, not truthful enough, it can be seen that their likeness extends past their literary excursions. A comparison of sitting portraits of the two authors shows a striking resemblance between them, which even the most sceptical of viewers could not fail to recognise. Both display large, overpowering foreheads; deep-set, melancholy eyes. Both mouths are crooked as if they had just overheard a humorous joke not meant for their ears. Even their dress is similar, those black ties, that white shirt. A scientific study conducted ten years ago, and published in a now-defunct Czechoslovakian journal of portrait physiology, analysed the composition of the two men's eyes relative to the central visual points of their faces. The similarities between the two sets of eyes were said to be so numerous as to defy reality. In an effort to explain the unsettling discovery, the study's authors discussed the possibility of the two writers having been identical twins. Though surely they must have known this was impossible, there being many years between the passing of Poe and the birth of Baudelaire. Unless, however, they meant it in another sense.

It is my suspicion, one which I can support with examples if anyone were to ask me (ha! and who would ask me anything, my poor neighbour?), that Baudelaire, in his efforts to surpass the literary similarities he had discovered between himself and his hero, altered his physical appearance to better match that of Edgar Allan Poe. I have read of similar cases in recent history, though none have been as extreme as this. Unfortunately I could find no photographs of the young Baudelaire from before Poe's spell had arrested him to test my suspicion. At the time no surgeon in Paris—the city I believe Baudelaire lived and wrote in for much of his life—could have been capable of such transformations, but Baudelaire is known to have spent some time in Germany, too. The purpose of these visits is obscured by Baudelaire: he would write that he had been, but the question of what he had done he never answered. It is interesting, then, to note that his visits occurred around the time of the publication of the surgeon Karl Ferdinand von Graefe's major work, entitled *Rhinoplastik*. This contains some wonderful histories on various plastic surgery techniques from times as far as the old kingdom of ancient Egypt. There is also an informative account of Graefe's own innovations to the genre. It must be remembered that this is just speculation; Baudelaire may have altered his appearance by any number of means.

I recount these snippets to lend credence to what I am about to reveal. The revelation of white bone during the rhinoplastic procedure must shock innocent onlookers—if these are still allowed inside the theatre. What follows may, too, shock; however, that white bone is entirely natural, and wholly necessary; without it the tunnel of the nostril would collapse, trapping air inside and out. And if the bone surrounding the mouth were to be removed, no more air would enter that body. The sight of bone must be shocking because it reminds us of what we are and what it is we need to be. My first introduction to Gesualdo was a documentary. A fifteenth-century Italian prince, the inspiration for Shakespeare's Macbeth, the composer of celebrated madrigals, the murderer of his son, his wife, and her lover, an evader of time and space: a man I will soon become.

The documentary unfurled a series of increasingly bizarre occurrences with the nonchalance of a street cleaner sweeping autumn leaves. Some sequences were especially striking. I have revisited these so often as to make them permanent fixtures in my imagination. In one, an enchanting flame-haired opera singer leads the cameraman on a chase through a Venetian castle before being cornered in the dank basement. She is the reincarnation of Gesualdo's murdered wife. When asked for her address, she replies:

Take a left at the chandelier in La Scala opera house in Milan. In the second row there is a box draped in red damask. That is where I live.

The next concerns a scholar who wrote his thesis on Gesualdo. After graduating with honours, he continued with his studies, attempting to expand his efforts into book form. He soon immersed himself in Gesualdo's life. He was American but began to speak Italian exclusively, despite having never formally learned the language. He scared his wife with hints regarding her unseen lover, muttering obscure words in his sleep. He was later found on their living room floor, his body transformed by thirty-eight stab wounds. A police officer—who had been the first on the scene, after the scholar's distraught wife—retired from his job and wrote a book about the experience. I visited the bookshop a while ago to read this but the writing was unappealingly pedestrian. The back cover quoted the following: "There was a nightmarish atmosphere in that house. The minute I walked through the door I felt like I was in somebody else's dream. I will never forget that feeling . . ." Or something to that effect.

As I wrote this, I was interrupted by the ringing of the doorbell. It was my next-door neighbour. Her washing machine had flooded and she could not afford to pay for a repairman. I was anxious to get back to my work, and was about to shut the door, but she insisted. She begged me to help her and I saw tears well in the corners of her strong blue eyes. I finished the work after dark, and after thoroughly cleansing myself, slept heavily.

I dreamed of Gesualdo and an Italian baker from the documentary who had told the cameraman over and over that Gesualdo was the devil. I dreamed of an Argentinian, Julio Cortázar. I dreamed he had previously written about Gesualdo: a story about a travelling group of singers who perform his songs, who find his essence insidiously creeping into their lives. Distraught, I must have cried in my sleep as I could taste the salt of my tears on my lips when I woke. I hurried out to the bookshop in search of his work. I found what I was looking for, "Clone." It was in the Spanish which I still cannot read. Yet, in the dream I . . .

A side story in an intriguing biography of Gesualdo depicts two men in a Milan asylum who each believed himself to be Gesualdo's reincarnation. Unfortunately this scant sentence, and one or two more detailing their supposed mental health, were all I could find about these two men. They may have suffered similar fates to the American scholar. All I know is their mental states were obviously such that they could not adequately deal with the rigours of daily life and so were secured in safer surroundings.

G. K. Chesterton believed the true artist was one who could exorcise his art without delay and resume the life of the everyday, ordinary person. It is only those who do not know how to produce art that find the artistic impulse a hindrance to their efforts to keep up with the everyday. He believed these unfortunate people exhibit what is known as the artistic temperament: "It is essential to every sane man to get rid of the art within him at all costs . . . There are many tragedies of the artistic temperament, tragedies of vanity or *violence* or fear."

If we were to suppose for a moment that Gesualdo's spirit did in fact come to inhabit the American scholar, and the two men in the asylum, it could be said that these men, rather than their suffering arising from a neurobiological origin, in fact suffered the fate of Gesualdo inhabiting their mind and body. It is well known that apart from his diabolic nature, he was a musical genius, two lesser-known facts were his practice of alchemy and his interest in the occult. From the limited evidence at our disposal and with reference to Chesterton, there are only two possible conclusions.

    (a) The artistic scope of Gesualdo's spirit was too much for the poor men whose bodies he came to live in.

    (b) It was the evil nature of his spirit which drove these men to madness.

I have been putting off this next part. This is where I reveal my role. I confess to having similar feelings to Baudelaire's reading of Poe, on my first reading a translation of Julio Cortázar's collected short stories. At first I thought little of it; there have been, and still are, so many people writing in this world across the centuries that it is inevitable that certain stories and phrases will cross time and place, landing in the pen of one man in one century and in the keyboard of another years later or before. Yet I have somehow written words and phrases which I later found in Cortázar. I cannot believe I was influenced by him as I had never read him until a chance visit to a bookshop during a business trip in a cold little English town saw me buy his translated stories. It is possible that he was influenced by writers I have admired, those whose writing has worked its way between my veins until it became my own. Yet, the coincidences are too many for such a simple explanation to fully suffice. When it came to the story of Gesualdo, Cortázar had gotten there before me. Obviously he has a head start on me as he died around the time I was born. But you could say I have an advantage over him as I am still alive, and so can choose to write about anything that takes my interest. Unfortunately he has, so far, pipped me to the post each time. I have come to realise there was something more to it.

Chesterton was aware of the mundanity of the spirit world, or as it is more commonly known, the alternative dimension. When he spoke of artists and temperaments, he was speaking of spirits and possessions. He knew there was only so much artistic spirit in the universe, and that it must necessarily travel from body to body, like a virus, in order to survive.

I suspect Cortázar has come to inhabit me, a part anyway, possibly my left hand, the one that makes vaguely Latin gestures as I talk, the hand I write with. Others have said that only the devil can flit between souls and that he is the source of all art. If that was so, then Cortázar the man was separate from Cortázar the writer, for the latter must have been the Devil. And if this is true, and I believe it to be, then the only possible conclusion from my above quandary must be option (b). Those men who were incarcerated for believing they were the incarnations of

Gesualdo simply could not cope with the inherent evil present in art. I believe I could. And I have done, for is this not art? And am I not still alive, still sane?

I feel at this stage I should apologise to both the Devil and to Cortázar. The art of Cortázar, though so much better than my own (if I can even lay claim to an art), is not good enough. He was apparently a kind and respectful person, if a little prone to melancholy. He played the trumpet, poorly, I hear. I want to be much more than that. I desire the talents and ambition of Gesualdo; with them I will finally produce art that will transcend myself. And when I die my spirit will be subsumed into that dark, amorphous thing that travels across the earth in search of bodies, of books.

Being impatient, I have sought to speed the process of inheriting Geusaldo's spirit. Having studied his portraits, I discovered his nose is aquiline. Mine was not. I tenderly touch the gauze above my lips. The pain tablets are working; it is as if I am touching putty wrapped in cloth. I cannot think of sneezing nor blowing it, and fear for the winter, but it should be healed by then, and if not, it is a small price. Our lips, once I shaved my thick beard (I suspect I have Cortázar to thank for that), I discovered, are exactly the same, as if we were carved from the same mould! But our eyes; unlike Baudelaire and Poe, mine and Gesualdo's eyes are very different. His are blue and so strong they could pierce through time. Mine were two brown muddy pools.

The old lady's washing machine continues to leak through the walls. I have not yet looked in a mirror on account of the stitches (for now, I see only through my fingers and the keyboard). I have no doubt these measures will speed up the process considerably. Her eyes were the perfect shade of blue, so piercing, her tears were waves entreating me to their depths. So beautiful; she will be the subject of my first madrigal.

Theme on the Character and the Actor

CONSIDER THREE DEATHS: THE HISTORICAL assassination of the Roman Emperor Julius Caesar, the fictional recreation of that assassination in Shakespeare's *Julius Caesar*, and the assassination of Abraham Lincoln. Three principals feature. The first is Marcus Junius Brutus, the original political assassin. To avoid confusion, we'll refer to him by the name which Caesar is said to have uttered with his last, blood-drowned breath: Brutus. The second and third are among the greatest Shakespearean actors in nineteenth-century America: Junius Brutus Booth and his son John Wilkes Booth. There will be no attempts to round out their characters in order to empathise with them and/or better understand pivotal moments in history. Aspects of their lives will be discussed, but only briefly and in relation to events that are bigger than men. They will remain photographs, left in the sun for too long.

The centripetal force which propels these three principals and three deaths is a fictional character. It is the Shakespearean role of Marcus Junius Brutus. It is the spider at the centre of this web that manages, with its sticky strands, to pull together and compress vast tracts of time and geography.

This character contains aspects of the historical Brutus, for it is a role based on his deeds. These aspects may be psychological, or physical. We are made of atoms and molecules. They continue after we die and become parts of other things or beings until they die or are destroyed, and so on. It is not inconceivable that these particles have a sort of memory, or that they may gravitate to that which is similar to one of their previous structures: the role of Marcus Junius Brutus, played by both Junius Brutus Booth and his son John. This is one possibility. Another: popular psychology books state, "To be confident, you have to fake it till you make it." If this is true, then the minds of men who are paid to pretend to be other people must be questioned. I cannot, will not, provide answers. I can only provide two excerpts and a quote. The first was found in a letter from Junius to President Andrew Jackson in 1852: "You damn'd old scoundrel . . . I will cut your throat while you are sleeping" (he didn't).

The second is taken from the diary of his son John Wilkes Booth, a lesser actor but more successful assassin. It was written in 1865, days after killing Lincoln: ". . . I am here in despair. And why? For doing what Brutus was honoured for . . . And yet I, for striking down a greater tyrant than they ever knew, am looked upon as a common cutthroat." When John Wilkes Booth shot Lincoln, he repeated a line, first uttered by Brutus, that echoes through centuries and continents: "*Sic semper tyrannis*." It is a cursed line. Tyrants—those who treat men like puppets—are rarely defeated. In fictionalising the Roman assassination, Shakespeare fastened reality to fiction, creating a Möbius strip, a trap from which Junius Booth escaped. His son was less fortunate.

whiteroom

WHILE THE WINDOW IS LARGE and takes up much of the room's front wall, the inside is dark. The sun, situated so far from here, so much larger than here, neglects this small room. It has ignored this space almost angrily, as if this room or its inhabitants had once made fun of its appearance. When we had visitors—when? when we still lived as others still do—they would walk right through the room to its back door and into the kitchen. Rarely did anyone stay where we wanted without our insisting, despite the obvious comforts of our furniture, our welcoming posture. (The room was not always so bereft.)

To read—no, I finished that a long time ago. To be truthful, I reread: memories of words rise and return to old forms: my books are of ghost stories, and now that I think of it, every story is about ghosts, how could it be otherwise? To experience these, lamps must be turned on early in the day unless I sit right by the window, collapsed on the floor. That is uncomfortable. We have arranged the furniture so often, I am sure there was an armchair by the window at one stage, for at least ten years or longer, but now there is floor and a small Chinese cabinet, the top of which barely reaches the sill.

The window faces north on a wall fifteen feet wide. The remaining three walls are equal in measure. These are painted white: an empty storm of a colour, the colour of pure memory. It is within these walls that we most prefer to live. We being myself and the memories of my wife.

It is only I that manage to complete such tasks as rearranging the furniture, or adding another layer of white to the ceiling, walls, or floor, but she is not completely negligent. For instance, she points out missed spots—I am always missing spots, faded white is glancing when seen from a distance, but up close one white shade is much like another.

We prefer it when surfaces recede or disappear altogether, leaving a blankness of space through which we could, if it were something we might like to do, walk through, and walk in white until exhaustion pulled us down, slowly, to white. We do not choose to do this but it is something we could easily do. Once there is enough white we have the option. Equally, my wife might cease to exist in all that whiteness, whereas I would remain a dark stain.

In colour: a coffee-coloured leather sofa and two matching armchairs make up our largest furniture. Prancing around these heavies, *as my wife likes to say*, are one marble-based lamp topped by a silk shade, a Chinese cabinet for storing blankets (I think I mentioned that already), a nest of polished mahogany tables, three reading lamps of varying heights—all fashioned from copper and bought to order, an Indian rug, a fireplace of gray marble, a dark mahogany bookshelf. There are 150 books on those shelves. There are three blankets of knitted cream wool in that cabinet. Hidden beneath the sofa, inside the cabinet, in the fireplace, on the floor, are thirty buckets of paint: all white.

There are other rooms in our home. They are not like this.

I age dreadfully in those other rooms, even the hall that leads to the front door will weaken my step. We exist quite forever within the white.

*

I am just going outside.

*

My wife, sadly, died when she answered the door to a pizza delivery girl. The girl had the wrong address. My wife stepped

into the hall before I could stop her. It was as if her bones had
been blown away by the draft the way I found her on the floor.
I had said to leave the girl be. I even anticipated it would be a
case of the wrong address.

Or she did.

One of us said it wasn't for us. I am sure it was her. Then
why answer the door? She knew, as did I, as we had known for
so long now, to step across that threshold was to step closer to
death. I am just going outside.

Could she have tired of my company? Having no means of
paying for entertainment beyond the books in our shabby little
library, having exhausted topics of conversation bar the happen-
ings beyond the window, she might have taken those steps with
a total knowledge of what would happen, knowing she would
be free of our diminishing. And yet, her memories have stayed
with me. They could have left along with her ability to plan
for the future, her feminine intuition, those wiles, but no, they
remain in this room.

We still wonder about the sun. Somehow the moon always
takes time to peer inside like a not unwelcome neighbour. The
sun, however, has excommunicated us from its light. We talk
about the planets, the postmen, the ladies who walk their dogs
on the path outside. There is plenty to talk about really, enough
so you wouldn't kill yourself just to avoid talking about it all.
Maybe her mind went, maybe the room only preserves the body
while the mind trudges a predetermined route through this blind
blizzard, our whiteroom.

*

We believe the rooms of a home house many echoes, echoes from
the past and future. They bound from the least expected surfaces,
each one covered by another somehow and each one possessing
the quality of silence, of overbearing loudness, depending on
who happens to listen. I am witness to each and every one. They
can be deafening, but not wholly unwelcome.

*

She sunk by the shore: in the shallows. I have heard fatal accidents most often happen on your doorstep. On a long journey vigilance is most required at the moment you begin to feel safe, at the end, as the key sits in the lock, or just before, when the keys are sought in a pocket or bag, or when you answer the door to a misdelivered pizza.

I never discovered what was on that pizza. If it had been poison, would I have eaten it, knowing my wife would be dead within seconds of closing the door? I don't know. It depends. Did she undertake that journey knowing how it would end? It depends on her knowledge, her decision. Her memories keep that to themselves. The bigger questions would concern the girl, the poison, the motive.

*

Often my wife will ask what I am reading, and I will reply with the author's surname and number. We know our books so well we have devised this system, for instance, Hugo 7 would be *The Last Day of a Condemned Man*, for it is the seventh book we bought by Hugo. If our library were limitless, the number would be different, but not the name. I ask her what she is reading and she replies in kind, just last night she said: Woolf 3. I like to tease her and pick the book from the shelf—her memories could not handle the physicality—and quiz her; for example, what is the fifth word on the thirty-first page?

I am sure she is mostly right. My wife has an excellent memory. Before we shaped our eternity from this square room, she had been a doctor specializing in the brain. She could recall every discovered synapse, could map every known function to its often minuscule location within that fat mass. I loved her looks: glances, gazes, full-bore stares: she had wicked eyes. Eyes you could see through and through; those pupils, her in the centre of clear azure by two.

Her bodily departure deprived me of the opportunity to

indulge in that aging couples' game: the gentle riffing on the gradual loss of each other's looks. I lost my beauty with one swoop. Fell it was, as it must always feel. I do not have the option of a face, a body to behold, and hold. But I am left with her strongest attribute, those memories. From these I remake her daily. Sometimes I feel she is more alive now than the many years we lived in this white space.

It is not too problematic, I don't think. I would never complain, but I am under such pressure not to succumb to illness, or worse. I cannot leave this room for anything. I am afraid to think what might happen to her memories when I am no longer around to care. What happens to memories left to themselves? Do they drift in search of others, living things full of experience and such, or do they remain, warm spots of air through which strangers unknowingly, unwillingly walk? I cannot let either happen to her—memories have been so devalued.

*

She wants it whiter. We were discussing the tree outside and she mentioned the offensiveness of its greens. It was surprising to hear she had been putting up with this invasion into our whiteness for so many years. We discussed, or rather I discussed, reasons for this, childhood encounters with the colour, bouts of hay fever, school jumpers, and the like, but she would not respond. I wanted to know why she had not said something earlier. She said there had never been a good time to bring it up.

*

I don't want to white the window. Already the doors are so invisible I couldn't find them unless I sidle along the wall, hands flat against the white. The furniture has been white for at least three generations now. I white the cracks daily. She cannot stand the—

*

This morning there were three seagulls on the garden wall. We live far inland. My wife suggested a storm was coming, that it might be better to paint the window now before the wind threw something through it. A mass of wet green leaves, or even worse. I was afraid of the wind's ferocity . . .

*

Unlimited, forever white.

*

Did I mention the whitening of the books? Their pages painted over, all those black letters gone. Their bleached spines like horizontal discs in a greater spine: four of them lined against eternity. She started that.

*

Those seagulls were white! They carried the open sea, the sky in their feathers. Stormy scenes inside them. Sometimes I wonder if we aren't hidden among the folds of some great white bird's wing: a gleaming falcon. One black stain, a flea among all that.

*

Sometimes I think I am memories like her. I am so bleached by paint in these clothes that weren't even dark to begin with, which are almost invisible to me now. My hands certainly are. They disappear unless I focus on their being.

*

Silence broods over our white-walled room.

*

She wants me whiter. Her hunger—thirst—need—desire for white surprises me—the intensity all of a sudden.

*

Her memories surround me, goading me to disappear. Join with me in memory to white, she says. I have tried other ways. Believe me. I want to. I cannot remember a good reason not to.

*

*

It took many, many years, but it happened. (Little happened in between.) We are two memories in the whiteroom now. Slowly we go. Slowly forgetting. We drift through white. Through and through we drift, always remembering, always white.

*

There are others here. Memories of suns, of meteors shooting, etc., each one pregnant with pastness. And all of it here in our whiteroom with these walls a person could walk right through.

Winter Guests

A MAN IS STAYING IN the hotel during the winter months for an indefinite time. He is working on an academic article. Or I think he should be, mostly he can be seen sitting on the larger balcony, beneath a blanket, with his back turned to the hotel, or he is walking the corridors at night. It is a given, I suppose, that he finds it difficult to sleep. That he insists on keeping his balcony door open to the frankly unnerving perpetuity that is the sea suggests he does not fit beneath the noun of *insomniac*, but rather the adjective *obstinate*. I do not especially enjoy watching him, but he is alive, and that is always interesting.

There are floods nearby, and the sea's cold lips foam all day at large rocks that must have fallen from the cliff upon which our hotel so carefully sits. For a while he has been the only guest, but two more have arrived this morning. He does not yet know this; there is no reason for him to be informed of this: just because he was the only guest means nothing to the staff, of whom there are few. It is winter, remember.

He wears a bathrobe (one of his own) when he walks at night. He knocks on the doors, an insouciant rap of the knuckles, as he passes each one. It is difficult to know really how loud he knocks, or what he expects to be inside those empty rooms, whether he is hoping someone might finally wake, and open the door, and welcome him inside. I wonder now, is this his first visit? How might he have stayed here before? So many people have briefly spread out their lives in these rooms only to pack them up again and return to what they call real life. They say this to us. They say

this is not real life, and grin or laugh as they say so, as if we were
not really working but only pretending and really just trying to
reduce our living like them: eating and bathing and sleeping
and eating and drinking and bathing and reading and sleeping:
trying desperately to relax, to reduce their consciousness until
they lie at the level of the animal lazing in the sun; all this in the
attempt to reduce the friction inherent in living. Nobody ever
achieves this on their hotel break, and nobody wants to admit
it because that would be an admittance of a truism few want to
accept, especially on holiday. So they find they must still shift
their bodies every now and then so as to avoid discomfort in
bed at night, and as they lie on the sunbed, they must apply oil
to their limbs and torsos if they do not want to burn; they must
remove their clothes when it is late, and adjust the temperature
of the room so that they do not sweat or shiver, and must shower,
brush their teeth, perform ablutions, eat enough fibre, enough
carbohydrates, and so on; they must, in essence, continue to live,
and living, as anyone recently deceased will agree, is tiresome.
Yes, they assume we are not working, and I suspect we are not
even living things to them, we do not even struggle to relax like
them, there is no friction for us, because we are a part of the
hotel for the guests, interchangeable as those bricks which must
lie on top of each other smothered in plaster and paint to make
these walls. I know this because I, too, have stayed in hotels.

He spots the new guests in the dining room while he fills a
glass with orange juice. He is calm or pretending it, but when
he returns to his table, he frequently looks away from the book
he has propped against the vase, turning quickly, as if reviewing
the empty room, to glance at the others at a table on the far side.
One is attractive (our clientele often are—naturally, or they can
afford the imitation of beauty), the other is unknown. This one
sits in a wheelchair in a full-body cast with a small opening for
the face. From where I sit, that face is hidden in shadow. The
woman appears to speak tenderly to the other. Too tender to be
a relative, a daughter or sibling, and I dearly wish she is not the
mother, but no, as I have said, the way her fingers roam that
plaster speaks of the sensuous—as only fingers can; she must be

a lover to that unfortunate being. What misfortune could be the cause of that total encasement? I do not know. She is not so young, not so young that I would immediately suspect that unknown individual to have wooed her with riches. They must once have been equals, and now she is the carer. The man continues to glance across the room, though she does not appear to notice, and the other—only they know what they see. They: inside that cast their gender is unknown, I could say "it" but I would be speaking only of that (possibly) temporary skin. They are hidden, they might even be true to the plural: there may be two or more persons trapped inside, small captive children perhaps. I wonder, does she stroke that hidden face at night, in empty rooms, in silent corridors, how receptive that skin must have become to air, to touch. Whether the man is entranced by her beauty or intrigued by the unknown is, to me, a mystery. His table faces the sea and, if it were warm and lit by sun without, he would see in the reflection of the window those two guests among the bare tables. In the dull light all that can be seen is gray water flecked with white. He wears a soft Oxford, dark chinos, worn leather moccasins.

A few years ago the tidal wave washed so much of this coastline. It decimated so many lives as if they were germs inhabiting an otherwise clean surface: the palm of a hand, for instance. At this height, our hotel was safe, along with the staff, the guests, the travertine tiles, the vintage liqueurs, the glass walls from where those waves could be seen rearing and rearing as if they would never stop growing (growling). The dead came back to us that day, carried by the sea into our lives. A local man, who would often drink in the hotel bar along with his associates (who still do in the summer season), woke in his bed to find the most recent of his victims floating against the wardrobe. The unfortunate soul had been killed over a drug deal, so I heard, and was buried somewhere between the town and the sea. He had been missing for a few weeks before the arrival of the waves. Finding his dead victim returned and lying floating by his bed was enough reality for that local man. It was as if he had said, I am finished with the things of this world, and being unable to leave out of some impulse, or lack thereof, he escaped inside the multifold cities of the mind where he must have lost himself, because I have not seen him around here since, and have heard he is now cared for by his old mother. Poor woman. The waves must have lifted the earth and, seeing the dead man, carried him back to his last contact with life.

It would have been better if the uprooted man had been washed into an armchair, so that when the woken man, the local assassin, groggily entered his sitting room in the morning, he would see the top of a stranger's head, resting, as it were. Carefully taking his gun from his waistband (he is the sort who must always carry a hidden, unlicensed weapon) he decides to surprise this rude intruder and see what it is he wants before shooting him. He jumps in front of the chair, gun raised, and sees the grinning (they always grin) face of his last victim. I would have preferred if the story had unravelled like that, but no, it wasn't half as interesting. The teller finished her telling with a joke about sleeping with the fishes, so perhaps she herself had twisted the story to suit her quip, and so really I should have told my more intriguing, and yes, classic, version of the story, as I am sure now it would have been truer than her version. He found the dead man sitting in the armchair, with a book which had fallen onto the lap, no, a newspaper, opened to the report of the victim's disappearance—that's what happened.

The woman dresses as if she were at a garden party in the grounds of some large villa. The man's eyelids flicker when she walks behind his table in the evening—I am certain I hear those heels against that marble—and he turns the page of his book then, before turning it back some seconds later, and remains on that initial page for another few minutes. I suspect this turning of the page before he has finished is the result of an urge to do something, an impulse to assert his being at that moment, to wake himself from the dream of another so that he may enter into the dream of someone still living, someone who might be a product of his own dreams, someone he hopes to translate from those dreams to his memories. Yes, I believe he is no longer working on his academic article. I have seen him with pages and his laptop just the once, now he only carries a book with him as he moves through the hotel. I have been told it is an Agatha Christie: *At Bertram's Hotel*, which is fitting considering his surroundings. Often he walks and reads and trips on the rugs, throwing his arms holding the book out in front of him as if he were trying to dive through the floor, the book somehow providing an opening, a sinkhole through which he might disappear. He is never injured. I cannot speak for his feelings, his thoughts; these are much easier to hide.

The lobby is four stories high; many visitors have said it is cavernous, some have even referred to it as cadaverous—which is fair. It is the heart of this hotel, and that metaphor is not a careless one, because the plans, which are encased in glass by the lifts, reveal its shape to be vaguely that of a heart; this similarity is underlined and elaborated upon in the bronze sign fixed below the casing. Corridors leave and enter the lobby in a manner deliberately reminiscent of the circulatory system, with more corridors opening on the third floor onto the upper balcony which overlooks the lobby on all sides: these, I am guessing, are the arteries—my knowledge of the inner body may be wanting, but I know my hotel.

A reclusive, but celebrated, artist was commissioned a number of years ago to paint a canvas to match the scale of our lobby. She painted a veritable *Guernica*: it is immense—four panels of thickened paint coloured, shaped, and styled to represent this hotel, and this cliff, and the sea, and the sky which had been hiding in the background all that time. In the first of the panels the hotel is much as it is now, though changed slightly: it appears to teeter on this cliff more than is possible. Its age is more pronounced, as if she were finding its true character: the one beneath the tan and the sunglasses, the dyed hair. The second panel depicts this hotel ravaged by some unseen force. The north wall is collapsed, opening its emptied rooms to the wind and a furious spitting rain. It is distressing to see the many curtains so useless. In the third panel the hotel has vanished, revealing the bare and surprisingly smooth surface of the cliff: this panel resembles historical images, captured when we were not yet here.

In the fourth panel the sea and the sky are left alone to battle for the horizon. Looking closely, as I often do, in some parts, the sky can be seen to push onward down against the sea, and in others, the sea can be seen roaring up into the gray, its waves flashing white like the smoke of great guns. In all, as seen from a slight distance, the story of this panel can be discerned at once; there can be no winner, and no loser, the sky and the sea will fight each other until some greater calamity finishes them both. They are like paintings seen in a dream, brought over into waking life. There was supposed to be a fifth panel which would complete the sequence, however it was absent when the trucks transporting the other four arrived. The artist did not return our calls or answer our correspondence, and so we were forced to make do not knowing who would win that battle, or what terrible occurrence might defeat both the sky and the sea. Did that painting not survive the journey from dream to life? Perhaps the dream itself consisted of five stages, and as they progressed it became a nightmare and at the end, just before waking, was where the artist discovered the final panel.

The man passes through there on his nightly walks. He glares at the paintings. How? His manner I can only compare to that of a man in a nightclub who sees a more attractive, more successful, younger man standing close to a woman he still loves (so close their torsos touch), holding her hair in his hand as he whispers in her ear. It is as if he is envious of those panels. His posture stiffens, his arms swing heavier, his chin rises millimetres lifting lidded eyes that pretend that those panels are not so big, that they are not even worth pausing to admire, and he disappears once again into the long and twisting arteries of my hotel.

On the day the panels were revealed, local newspapers complained. Those at the opening had not stayed long. The artists had sent a letter, apologising, saying there had been a bereavement in the family and so they could not make it. Ever since the paintings went up, there have been complaints from the guests that these images frighten their children. Those who complained were informed that we, the hotel, do not assent to the fears of children or adults. And when they continue, whining and threatening to leave us, we ask whether they really believe a series of paintings are powerful enough to exert a force such that something dreadful will happen to this hotel and its occupants. Nobody has provided a satisfactory answer. Nobody wants to display their superstitions in the light for fear of what they might see.

The woman appears from a corridor slowly pushing the wheelchair and its stiff occupant into the lobby. I imagine the slow squeak of those wheels. She positions the person in the wheelchair in the middle of the room, facing the four panels. She caresses those plaster-of-Paris shoulders and whispers something into that opening before strolling away down another corridor. It would be easy now to suggest a connection between this mystery in white and the pursuit of ultimate relaxation. It might even be a service available only for the very wealthy, which would make that woman an assistant to the customer encased inside that stiff outer skin. I can only imagine the pure ease the muscles might achieve with no other option but to lie arrested in position. I do not think I have ever allowed myself to fall fully limp, life has denied me that, but this person, this mysterious customer is free to slacken every inch of their body. Something that occurs only beneath the influence of the strongest drugs, or in the sleep of the innocent (and what adult is innocent? *chuh!*), or moments after death. That is luxury. Perfect luxury. Envy luridly paints me. The woman must have been chosen for her beauty, in fact, now I think of it, the picture of her face is twinned in my mind with an Italian fashion house—she must be a model of some sort. She must care for the customer's every need. Whoever it is inside that cast I envy them. I wonder what the thoughts of someone so relaxed must be, I imagine them soft and malleable like their muscles, ponderous, rolling things: only someone who can think like that could leave themselves to the mercy of those four panels when the wind throws the rain against the windows of the lobby so angrily. (It is that peculiar species of rain so often found on the coast: shoals of it rush against the glass.) What if the power of the panels suddenly arrested that person's every thought? Because they can do that. The awful suggestion created by those panels often dawns on our customers days after their arrival. I cannot remember it ever being an immediate under-standing, they are too large, and the eyes too small, for that.

The man enters the lobby wearing a red blazer over a white linen shirt, and white chinos. He pauses by the reception, turn-ing the pages of a leaflet describing an attraction open only in the summer season, glancing now and then at the figure in the centre of the lobby. He strides toward it, bends over the person in the wheelchair, who now looks very small. The man is shouting into the small opening to the face, his hands grabbing at those stiff shoulders. He really looks inside now, and pauses. He appears to be listening to something the obscured person is saying, then, as if overwhelmed, he reaches an arm across the back of the figure and wrenches the person toward him so that this mockery of a relaxed, reclined posture falls off their chair to land squarely on their side on the floor. The man spits at this poor rich person, and walks back in the direction he came from. The person in the plaster cast appears unperturbed. Where the face should be it is still dark, and I wonder if they are so relaxed that they have accepted this violence, perhaps they are even sleeping. It is so difficult to know when they are so still and covered over.

The woman arrives and seeing her customer sitting sideways on the floor, arms and legs pathetically imitating comfort, runs and quickly rights the mystery into their chair and begins to wheel them away down another corridor. They don't speak, at least not that I can see. Just before they leave, she turns abruptly and stares at the panels, the way one would stare at an enemy when anger has moved all possible words out of reach.

In the morning, a member of staff notices that wheel-chair-bound mystery sitting at the bottom of the outdoor pool, sans wheelchair. After calling for help, possibly fearing the per-son inside could not still be breathing, but possibly optimistic considering the calm seated posture of the cast, he dives in and drifts the white body to the surface where he edges it onto the poolside. There appears to be no face inside the small opening at the top through which to breathe life-giving air. The staff mem-ber feverishly rolls the cast on its side and it gives way more easily than he seems to expect, though it is heavy, due to the water, and the dead, it seems. He turns it upside down, and onto its other side, running his hands over the plaster, searching for an opening, panic speeding his movements. His hands return to that palm-sized opening where the face should be. They reach in past his wrists. A sealed tomb, someone later said. More staff members arrive, and one carefully cuts the cast in half. Most of the staff, it seems, are now standing around the shape where a body should be. In its place is a congealed mass of paint differing in texture, colour, and density, covering the whole of the inside—some of it has run with water from the pool. As the staff watch, wondering, I imagine, what to do or say, the cast flattens out, like a tired piece of origami, revealing the fifth, and clearly the final, painting of the series. The staff turn as one to glance back at the hotel. Two paramedics emerge, and jog toward them. The staff slowly, reluctantly it seems, make an opening in their circle for the two who step forward. Nobody speaks.

*

In the centre of the lobby the wheelchair lies on its side. In the dining room the man sits with a page taken from his room on the table before him. A few words lie at the top of that page, illegible. On the floor are two halves of a pencil. The woman cannot be seen.

Haircut

APPARENTLY, NO HAIR HAS EVER grown on the palms, the soles of the feet, the lips, never in all our years. That skin is glabrous. What is left of the body is mostly covered in either thick terminal, or fine downy hair. The finest strand is very thin: about thirteen micrometres: no thicker than a thread of spider's web doubled by dew—just before the droop, I think. I remember reading about a gland found at the opening of each hair. It produces a fatty secretion that lubricates the hair, that prevents it from dying.

I had not been to the barber for four years. My reasons are not uncommon (small talk, sport talk, pop songs). As always, there was something else, too, just beyond my understanding (. . .). When I finally went he was not there. The door opened at my push. The stairs were steady under my steps. The radio was banal. The barber was gone. The air was hot outside, hot even for midsummer. Weather for people to enjoy, or do their very best to.

I asked for him in the hairdresser's two shops down, in the belief there must be some link between the two professions. The girl said he could no longer do it. I asked if she could. She said she would, but quickly; it was almost closing time.

*

I watched my hair fall to my cape-covered arms and my knees, where I jiggled it to the floor. I puffed upward when it landed on my nose, blinked furiously when a strand balanced on my eyelashes. Too many hairs. So much. I hate when a man with a shaved head sits in front of me on the bus. The number of shorn black dots is so dizzying I have to look down at my hands to stop the nausea. It repulses me somehow, the knowledge that there are so many.

In preparation for my haircut I had avoided reading those sentences that estimate the number of hairs a person has, but now, seeing them fall I found myself wanting to know how many might grow on the average head. I needed to know this, and on the average person, too, counting especially those downy strands unseen by all but the most thorough lover. My hairdresser guessed at least a million on one head, multiple millions all over: her hands navigated a vague map illustrating each possible location on her body. My eyes followed with a tourist's keen attention. I wanted to ask her other questions.

I wanted to feel words in my mouth. She spoke about Nikola Tesla: "I read the other day that Nikola Tesla had a fear of hair. He refused to touch anyone's hair, his included. He had a fear. To say he had a fear is to say he owned it: it wasn't a primal thing like being afraid, it was distant from him, like a hobby. He chose fear for a hobby. He chose as his fear one of the few things a human cannot escape, the hair that grows from almost every inch of their skin. I respect that, even if I find it ludicrous. In my opinion, hair should be trampled on, destroyed." She ran a hand over the smooth skin of her head as she said these last words. There was a caution, a submerged panic, in her movement that I didn't understand—not that I tried, instead I wallowed in the course of her strange thoughts. They were rare, rib-eye steak–like thoughts, luscious and wrong somehow. I tasted them, slowly, silently.

*

We were alone in the shop—if two people can be that. Almost finished. She undid my cape and flicked my neck with a soft-bristled brush. She puffed a powder about my head then made some finishing snips. "How many hairs do you think I cut off your head just now?" she asked, gesturing with the open jaws of her silver scissors. The radio had been off for some time. I looked down at the scattered black strands that minutes ago had grown from my head. I glanced around: the row of empty chairs beside me looked like each should be surrounded by clear Perspex walls, straps on each arm. I suddenly felt foolish for having trusted her to run those scissors through my hair, to scrape that razor along the skin of my neck. Her thoughts repeated on me, returning misshapen and tasting of bile. Fully aware of my propensity for alarm, and of the nature of this world, which means that any moment can become the last moment without reason or explanation, I strove for calm, and studiously brushed at hairs that had escaped down the collar of my shirt, then bent to evacuate a handful of hair hiding beneath the cuff of my left trouser leg.

barber . . .

young gentleman . . .   being in liquor . . .

a fine girl in Hamilton Street . . .   had had certain favours the night before . . .

the barber,

his wife . . .

in a frenzy . . . cut the gentleman's throat from ear to ear . . .

These fragments swam before me, carried, no doubt, from some distant memory, by the wave of blood rushing, breaking on attention's shore when I bent. I stood up, too quickly; a dizzying tiredness came over me. A tiredness innocent Samson must have felt by the end of his story. Darkness crept. I collapsed back into the chair as if the roof were falling in, my head falling against the stitched leather back.

At once I felt madly sorry for my hair. Tears overflowed my lacrimal lakes—those hidden reservoirs of sorrow found in books on anatomy, and just beside the eyes, which might as well be oceans. But hairs are simply a nuisance to be dealt with, inefficient once their number increases past a certain border. I thought I had thought that. Greasy unless frequently washed. That's what I had thought. Forget them. That's what I would do. But.

"What happens to them?" I asked.

"They are sold to make wigs for bald children. Or burnt, I don't know," she said from over by the counter. She took a sip from a flask, or a mug.

I looked again at my hairs scattered on the shop floor. If my body were a country I would be its cruel government, the tyrant hidden in bulletproof convoys, in hilltop castles, its cufflinked austerity. And my hairs. My defenceless hairs lying where they had fallen. What would they be? The disabled, the defenceless poor; burnt, or made into wigs for bald children.

But this has always happened. Nobody escapes the encroaching past. They must be swept away with the dirt and the— Dust begets dust. There will always be more, I imagine. I imagine those children: innocent. Is it innocence when you are unaware, innocent to benefit from the unethical: the second- or third-hand murder, the fifteenth? Nobody could blame them. Growing up with their borrowed hair they learn too late. How many hairs have I willingly had decapitated in my life? Not as many as some—I can say that, at least. I could change. There is almost always time for change.

I closed my eyes and pretended to sleep, and tried desperately to think of a way to save those hairs. I found the night inside me. No thoughts or feelings, no brilliant plans, no remembrance of her and her delicate hands tracing her downy map, though I sought that image in every dark corner. No. Thoughts slouched from some murky swamp, yes, be careful now, but she had disappeared from my mind. The room was silent. I waited.

I strained to hear the sweeping. Instead I heard their clamouring—galloping now! I opened my eyes, just a little; she stood behind my chair. We remained like that for at least ten agonising minutes, maybe more. My watch ticked off each slow second, though I could not hear for the thundering.

I could take it no longer, and jumped up, and asked why she

had not swept my hairs away. It was getting late, I said, and the shop was supposed to be closed by now: "You said so when I came in, didn't you? You said it would have to be a quick cut."

"I've been thinking," she said.

"You're not paid to think, you are paid to cut and dispose of my hair!" I shouted. In the mirror my face had become red; veins stood out on my forehead. "Remove these immediately!" I kicked at a clump of hair that had probably sat ungainly above my ear.

She said nothing.

It had turned to silence now. Closing in. It burrows down and finds more of itself inside me and there is an erosion of the already softening edges of myself until: "What are you thinking about, what is it?"

"Hair, mostly."

"Well, say something, then, tell me your thoughts, you spoke enough before? Say something!"

"I was thinking about how funny it is. This business. We are executioners, you know, you do know that . . ."

I was silent, a white wall enclosed by an absence of colour and noise. Overwhelmingly captured. We are executioners, you know. I rolled her words on my mute tongue, waiting: youknow, youno, escution r, wexcutin yuno—

"We are executioners and you are both customer and victim. We have been decapitating living tissue for so long now. Once, hair grew to a standard length just like your arms or ears." That sweep of a hand across her scalp again.

"In my country, youngsters were sent into the wilderness when puberty and its hair began to transform their bodies. If they survived this journey, they were to return first to the hair-cutter's home, usually built on the outskirts of the village. Over seven days the haircutter would cut and remove every strand of hair. Completely hairless they then returned to the village to be welcomed as a member of the community, as an adult. At the end of the year, a festival was held, the culmination of which was the burning of the year's hair."

"Did it, did it ever grow on the palms, on the soles of our

feet, on our . . . our lips?" I asked, certain I would die if I heard the answer, that I would die if I did not ask.

She may have replied, I am not sure (yet I still live). She said much more about the festival, about the annual harvest, and rites that sounded like descriptions of medieval woodcuts, but when I try to recapture it in writing I cannot. I could create what she said, but that would be lying. (In fact, I just now tried that—there is nothing there.)

In truth, it was soothing to have such a voice speak to me, the only one in that room, to have it ring loud and running through my ears like children on a Saturday morning on a warm day like it was. People walked past on the pavement outside, and I, briefly free, watched them, stared at their clothes, a particular gait, one especially, how he reminded me of . . .

"Now, hair does not cease, every day the hairs reach a little farther from the skin, in search of survival, freedom. It holds secrets . . . It grows seventy-six percent faster today than it did a hundred years ago. It grows when you are dead: the ultimate one-upmanship: it survives you despite your regularly paying for its decapitation, your smothering it in shampoo and conditioner." She took a long-bristled sweeping brush from a far corner and slinked toward me, trailing it across the floor behind her.

"Now you understand," she said.

I understood less than ever, gathered money, enough to include a tip—probably far too much—dropped it on the counter and ran out into the evening air. Even outside I could hear the long passes of the sweeping brush, the shushing, and the pushing; and the silent, dead hair.

Passing by the window of the butcher's shop, my face looked different, lighter. I would have bought meat for a barbeque, but they were closed, and I was glad. I felt very tired.

Skin

ONCE, WHEN I WAS VERY young, my father brought me to the circus. This is not an unusual experience for a child, and as far as I could tell there was nothing unusual about this particular circus, though never having been again, I cannot be sure. There were clowns and a ringmaster, elephants and other animals, too, and all those other aspects without which a circus loses its claim to that name. I am writing this because I saw a man in that ring whom I cannot forget, and I hope that by transferring these thoughts to words, he will become more distant than the passage of time has achieved, and perhaps these words, so rigid and upright, will trap him somehow and leave me free of one more unwanted memory.

His skin was so thin I could see veins crawl through his smiling face, his neck, his arms. Even his fingers, when held against the light, reminded me not of my father's fingers, nor those of any other man I had known, but of dead fish frozen by ice. Living next to a hospital, I had seen disfigurement, but those afflicted people have not stayed with me. Certainly none have caused me to wake in the night decades after seeing them. Maybe it was because I often saw those people sitting in the cafe eating breakfast after a long drive for an early appointment, heard their celebratory tones as they spoke with family members, or the solemnity of their disappointment, when I passed on my way to school, or it was just that they hadn't had lights shining so brightly on their skin, hadn't stood before an audience presenting their wounds. I'm not explaining it well—how can you explain what you don't understand? Whatever it was, this man—who he was, what he did—I had never seen anyone like it.

He is the only reason I remember this event, and, perhaps, the reason I have avoided every circus since. My memory circles his image in a way that recalls those red stripes spiralling toward the tent's pointed ceiling. When I saw him I wanted to rescue him and urge him toward the hospital, but I was just a child in an audience—a participant.

I imagined his too-visible veins were roots that had grown up through one of his feet, or had snuck through his back as he lay asleep in some field, roots that had secretly overgrown his body, sucking the good from food so that he grew thin. He was very thin. I was worried those veins would burst through his skin at any moment. I am sure I saw buds and green shoots beneath that seeming translucent skin. That unfortunate man. The ringmaster had called him by some obviously made-up name and left him alone in the ring.

I am haunted by this man. I constantly relive his act, stretching what can only have lasted a few minutes into a horribly misshapen thing that has bridged all these years. These moments live inside me and refuse my understanding, and so I live with them. It is always those that we think of as bad memories that seem so resilient, and I wonder if it is because they pose a puzzle to us: we cannot understand something about them, perhaps it was an aspect of our behaviour that resists our understanding, something we did that won't fit our image of ourselves no matter how hard we try to reshape it, or it is the behaviour of another that we fail to comprehend, another's behaviour which reveals the world as something other than we had previously imagined, and we cannot bear to accept this new understanding, and so the memory follows us, taunting us until we break and make space for this new world.

When I looked again the man had folded his arms around a small sheet, as if cradling it. I gasped when I saw that sheet was his skin. He had somehow stretched the skin of his upper arms and held each one in the opposite hand. From his grin, it was clear that this was not unusual to him, that he knew this was what the audience wanted. He suffered no physical pain. I am sure I said something to my father about feeling ill and wanting to leave at that point, but he appeared transfixed and mumbled some words I cannot remember. The lights dimmed. Drums rolled (their echo still rolls through these bones). There was a burst of sound and a lady appeared in the spotlight, high up near the ceiling.

But this was of no interest to my young self. Instead, I watched the man below. He waited in the dark. He remained absolutely still. He was a tree without leaves; the only one, in a dark field, far from any of those homes with their smug yellow windows—those members of the audience sitting in those rows surrounding him. Untouched by life, not even the wind. I was entranced by the skin that bridged his arms, how obscene it was, how he held it. The despair of the artist in darkness. Poverty's scythe always just behind and slicing. Society's scythe always just behind and . . . He was so unlike the fathers of my friends: they played their adult roles so well that I could never see the young boy inside—behind, or wherever youth goes to make room for age. But it was too easy to see that thin man out there in the dark as a child. I saw him running home from school, wiping at tears, running to his bed where he tenderly wrapped his loosened skin over and around his young body, creating a warm cocoon of self. Was he bullied for this affliction, this affliction become talent, was this nightly exhibition his revenge?

The audience gasped as a trapezist and the lady unfolded themselves from the trapezist's high perch, and swung across our heads, his legs somehow grasping the swing; his hands holding onto her slim ankles, leaving her arms free.

The thin man stood so still and alone, and this reinforces my belief that he was slowly becoming a tree. I see his toes buried in sawdust—how deep did they root? I stared into the centre of the ring, trying to understand his expression. Trying to see his past, see his family, how did they react to this son and his skin? Or was it something carried from the father to him?

A circle of light yanked him from the darkness. His face looked horribly eager: a man happy to be skin and bone. The audience wanted nothing from him but elastic skin and he wanted to give them as much of it as possible. I think what made me want to run home and curl up in bed away from my thoughts was the realisation that he found something within this degradation to enjoy.

Or was it not degrading to someone like him? Like him? I had no words for it at the time, but translating my young thoughts, I suspect I saw him as a person, a delicate, teetering person like anyone else, and I hated him for that. I, a child, who worried about the feelings of worms and of those belonging to little plants, too, I wished this thin man would cease to exist, wished he had never been born. (And, I suppose, people would say he did not deserve to be the focus of such thoughts.)

Far above us, the trapezist and lady swung through the tent, and white birds followed as if they, too, were fixed to a swing, and more birds, local birds, crows and magpies—indistinguishable from the dark ceiling when the spotlights veered away from them—they, too, followed that swing, cawing and spreading damp autumn night from their wings.

Flying to and fro, the lady shouted to the thin man and he shouted up at her from down below. I couldn't hear what they were saying, but the audience, including my father, laughed at their every utterance. I tried to focus on the sawdust closest to me, on the man behind the drum in the shadows near the entrance of the ring, anywhere but the pantomime in front of me. At some point, the lady began flinging peanuts at the thin man's skin, and he would angle himself so that they bounced into his mouth. I found this utterly frightening.

But more than that, it seemed to be the most crushing thing I had ever experienced (and now when I think of it, or dream of it as often happens, I feel, I think, the same). If despair were a body of water, I would have sunk down to the deep floor of it. And when my father glanced in my direction to share his enjoyment, I could not but quiver a weak smile back at him.

The shouting grew frantic, so frantic I was afraid the man's throat would burst open and expose those roots with their tingling leaves. Even the skin of the beating drum it seemed might explode in those charged moments. I must have covered my ears, as the memory now takes on a muffled quality.

When I next looked up at the swinging pair, the trapezist and the lady, she was pulling back the pocket of a sling-shot. I winced as the peanut pinged off the man's skin. It pinged! The most horrible sound, and yet I hoped to hear it every time because the absence of that ping would mean the peanut had broken through his stretched skin, and no matter how hard I hated, I did not want that. And when she missed, the thin man's eyes grew so wide I worried they would fall from his skull. I turned around in search of reason, mercy. People in the audience behind me wiped their eyes, flung their heads back—they roared laughter, revealed fat molars and pink throats. I was sure I was going to faint if I did not leave, but there was no place for me to go. I was as trapped as that man was inside his elastic skin. Just as I am trapped in this mind with this memory.

The show continued, as it must, with shouting that became ever more discordant. No longer were the skinny man, the lady, the trapeze artist smiling: flatly grim lips on all of them. I heard each ping, and despite the change in the performer's moods, the man continued to angle his skin so that the peanuts fired into his mouth, surely slamming against his delicate upper palate.

The audience gradually stopped laughing, and, through my horror, I felt a discomfort in the seats around me. But the show wasn't over yet. We had paid for our tickets. Value had not been had, not yet. The lady snatched a bulging bag from one of the perches and, reaching into it, produced an apple. She hurled it down, and I . . .

If I could have travelled back in time and sat beside my young self, I would have taken his head and cradled it in my arms, and carried him outside to the air with the sky above the trees, to gaze and breathe beneath those unceasing stars. The tent and its horror would grow distant and muffled. But the past is sealed. We cannot change what has already happened. We can choose only the angle from which we look back, and if we try hard enough, if we look from every possible angle, we might finally find the one where our view is almost completely obscured, and only then can we begin to forget. We cannot change the past, but it is always acting on us. I cannot remove my young self from that circus. Instead, he leads me, again and again, back inside that tent and up to that seat, leads me to witness these scenes, as if to say, Tell me now, with all that knowledge, all those years, tell me, what does this mean? All I want is to leave him there, to remove his hand from mine, and without looking back, without thinking very much, walk away, walk away from that insistent need to know.

Entrance to the Underworld

THE WOMAN POINTED AT THE page: "He needed to write the phrase a *bottomless pit*, you see?" I could not: the words were illegible from repeated folding, the paper thin and giving way, revealing the dark wood of the table behind those crossed indentations. The text, however, did not require reading to understand the mind it had come from. I mostly remember a dense writing trudging across the page, paragraphless, opening toward the bottom right of the paper, like the mouth of a harbour, or a cave. It was near the end of this writing, on the edge of its lower jaw, that she had pointed to. A bottomless pit. I nodded, and yawned into my fist. It was late.

But I was glad to have company. We had met after dinner. I had been reading a book of short stories from the hotel library (three surprising shelves) when she sat down next to me. By then, lamps had lit the room leaving plenty of darkness along the ceiling, beneath the tables, in the corners and the creases, so that I had to hold my book at an awkward angle to see its words. And I may have slept a little: in that low light we were not obliged to be entirely awake and instead could waver, with discretion, from one state to another: she may have woken me from a preparatory nap before bed, and, if so, I was glad that she did. She had come to the hotel in search of her missing brother, a writer. I was there for reasons I would prefer not to mention. Aside from the tall, and irritating, waiter, and the quiet man behind the bar, we were alone among the slow notes of Chopin's Nocturnes (to create atmosphere, I imagine). We had spoken, at first, about the book in my hand, written by an Italian, Dino Buzzati, whose name, we agreed, was pleasing to pronounce, reminding us both of bees and summer; this soon led to the subject of her sibling. I believe it is one of the laws written by grief—which are just as sure as those authored by gravity—that I could have said anything and her conversation would still fall toward him. For her, everything could not but lead to him, to his absence.

"And I know my brother, it is clear he needed to write the words—*bottomless pit*—and I am sure that the more he thought of that phrase, the more he suspected its veracity. As do I," she said. "Having committed himself to sincerity since the occurrence of a family tragedy—one that affected us in markedly different ways—he refused to allow anything false into his work. The need to write this phrase, this *bottomless pit*, was a hindrance to him; it was completely necessary for that sentence I showed you, I believe this, knowing the style of my brother as I do his face and voice, yet, to his mind, that phrase was unknown; likely false. One of those phrases that exists only as language, referencing only itself, whatever link it might once have had with truth worn away by time. I imagine he hated that he needed this phrase to be true, but knowing my brother, he had to test it. He could not write it otherwise, and yet it was the only phrase he could use in that sentence, this I know. The deepest human instinct is to wage war against the truth: he wrote this in his notes, which I plan to have published."

She described, with horror, the state of his abandoned hotel room (which did not sound all that worse than my own; however, there was no space for me to say this, and even if there were, I suspect she would have laughed at the thought). From her description, our rooms differed mostly in her brother's pinning on the wall above the writing desk pictures of sinkholes: glossy ones from magazines, and ghostly ones printed in poor quality and black and white. Many of these images portrayed the otherwise quiet of residential streets with captions acknowledging a swallowed car, or pet, a garden wall. Yellow safety tape and a rough mouth of tarmacadam often the only evidence of the ground's sudden hunger. I have studied those photographs, she said, examined them for clues of the chaos that is hidden beneath their surface. She described other pictures revealing older openings, edges cracked with age, in desolate landscapes admitting no sign of civilisation.

I had never seen a sinkhole, and had rarely thought of them, but as she elaborated, they struck me as incredible—mouths appearing in smooth flesh, or were they wounds? (and what type of wound opens from the inside?) yes, sinkholes belonged to that category of nature from which monstrosities such as lightning, tornados, and tidal waves erupt—vengeful-seeming things. It was frightening to think of them, though that fear did not stop, only encouraged, perversely, a vision I had of the thick carpet beneath us suddenly falling away, revealing an absence in the ground, and us falling, still in our chairs, the table still between us, our glasses falling beneath their liquid, while I continued to listen, and she continued to speak, even as our lives had been irreparably changed, before we could even comprehend this change in the stillness of our falling. It could happen here as anywhere, if I was to believe her. I felt myself shiver, and asked if she had any of these pictures to hand. She said she would bring some down the next night.

"I do want you to see them . . . it is so important to look," she said. "I remember a series of photos of a tooth from a gallery opening. A fat molar. The first photo was taken closely, against a plain white background, so that the tooth resembled a monolithic structure—one cleaned and removed from the earth by diligent workers. The other images were increasingly magnified, revealing geometric patterns, and dark shapes, which looked more geographical than biological, like satellite images of deserts and foreign cities—and all of this hidden within a few centimetres of smooth enamel, right on the surface. The world is everywhere to see if only we could look, don't you agree?"

I nodded, hesitantly. She continued: "And the world is rarely pleasant when seen like this; even that magnified tooth worried me, to think something like this protrudes from my gums—and there are so many of my teeth, how many living things must occupy all those alien ridges and cities inside that enamel! Others in the gallery pretended not to see this, even when I pointed out those features deep inside that tooth. And these, patrons of the arts! Yes, very few look too closely; they have learned to avoid it. They fear the world. My brother, however, was different. There were notes scribbled in the margins of those articles on sinkholes: What happened to the car!? Did nobody hear the noise when it hit the bottom of the pit? How deep? How deep? From these notes you can trace the slant of his thought. In a locked drawer in his desk, I found heavily underlined articles on sinkholes in the Yucatán Peninsula. Part of the peninsula is itself a pit," she said, "its having been crushed by an asteroid, the blast and debris of which would have rained across North America. Imagine, the heaviness of the sky falling on those poor dinosaurs." She smiled, as if this, the extinction of those creatures, were a private joke between us. The smile was left to fend for itself as she paused.

She thought very frequently, introducing these interludes where I felt she had retreated behind the curtain in preparation for the next scene while I was left to reflect on what had gone before, on the said. Left to order another drink, to glance at the book on my lap, to wonder if I should leave, to wonder if she was also lonely, and perhaps making up this story because she didn't know how to talk to a stranger yet could not but talk. I didn't really want to leave, not until *they* made me. And really, why should the extinction of the dinosaurs not be a little joke between strangers? Those powerful creatures would have been unmerciful toward us, I am sure of it. And even if she were making all of this up, the story was becoming true for her with each word, and in this way I saw the resemblance between her and the brother she spoke of.

"The problem was that my brother, in the course of his writing, had struck a rock, one which has forced greener writers to give up," she said. "And he was faced with that rock again in his searching: sinkholes must always end somewhere, at least the ones he read about. Oh, the disappointment he must have felt! and he had been reading the most romantic things about them. Did you know the Mayans called a sinkhole a *dzonot*? The closest translation I could find in English was 'abysmal and deep,'" she said, "though I cannot help but think of a donut, too. Is that very superficial of me? It must be related in some way to *dzonot* . . . he never liked them—preferred his cream cakes." She took a large drink of her vodka, and beckoned to the waiter for another for each of us. "Do you like the theatre?" she asked. "I'm sorry?" "The theatre, the roar of the greasepaint, and all that?" she said. "It's been a while since I've been, but yes, I suppose—" "It is likely you wouldn't have seen me, then . . ." She left a gap here, for once, but rather than smoothing it over with a well-placed, and flattering, question, I instead fell inside, and had to wait till eventually she came to my rescue.

"I played a Mayan princess when I was much younger. It was an awful play, very parochial, director with more ego than talent, you know the sort. But yes, I like to think I have a special insight into the Mayan mindset as a result. So you can believe me when I say I can perfectly imagine what it was like for the Mayans when part of the ground suddenly disappeared. A chasm." She snapped her fingers. "Just like that. In fact, they believed it was, and I quote this from my brother's research—so meticulous, he always was—the gaping mouth of a devouring earth god, or—listen to this one—the entrance to the underworld opened by Chaak, a god of life and water. Aren't they wonderful phrases? My brother must have thought so; he underlined these whenever they appeared in the articles, and he . . ." She reached a hand toward her handbag on the floor, then her hand—wavering, the diamonds on her many rings glittering against the dark—returned, empty, to the arm of her chair. "They had this chant: Chaak is one. Chaak is many. They would all chant this, led by their high priest or other whenever another *dzonot* opened, all of them, surrounding that great chasm, repeating their incantation until by this repetition they were not themselves but a part of something greater—hundreds of cells forming a supplicating body—free of their ordinary lives, free so that they might protect and prolong that ordinariness. Archaeologists had found golden objects, and human bones, placed in nooks or lying at the very bottom of these sinkholes and, as the openings filled with water over time, it became almost impossible to retrieve them, even now." She raised a page in front of her chest: CHAAK IS ONE. CHAAK IS MANY was written over and over, the words crawling among each other to create in the centre of the page a black confusion from which they crawled away again. A black sun, emitting the more legible rays of this phrase from its edges. When I reached out to take the page, she briskly folded it and placed it back in her bag, saying the paper was delicate, and anyway, there wasn't much more to see beyond those six words. She watched me very carefully as she said this.

She only learned her brother was living in this hotel in his last email. "He hadn't been in contact in months, and then he writes!" she said. "But he's always been like that." The email had been short. About needing to test something for truth and, if it survived intact—which he doubted—he had asked if she would retrieve his belongings from his room. I wanted to know if she was sure he was referring to the phrase *bottomless pit*, that that was what he needed to test? She looked at me in annoyance. "Whatever else could it be?" she said. On receiving the email she had immediately made arrangements to travel to the hotel. The receptionist said he had not been seen in a few days, that he seemed to spend much of his time away from the hotel, returning late when only the night porter might see him, and even then (here, she imitated the receptionist and, tapping the side of her nose, said) "the porter is aptly named, if you know what I mean." I said I didn't. She sighed, and said, "PORT?" I said: "Oh, of course, port, yes." She discovered her brother had bought a shovel in a hardware shop in the village. We parted before she could relay any more of her story. I invited her back to my room for a last drink and, to be honest, hear what her brother had done with that shovel, hear the end of it—I suspected it would be grisly, and I seem to be most susceptible to things of that nature early in the morning; she politely refused my invitation. Not feeling able for the agility demanded by the flight of stairs that stood between myself and my room, I took the lift. It brought me to a lower floor, and when I realised this and turned to press the correct button, I saw at the back of the lift a wall of faintly blue glowing water. I am sure I recoiled, as

I remember believing I was about to be engulfed, but the water remained behind the glass, and I saw I was on the threshold of the hotel spa—closed for the night. I returned to another floor, so much like the one I usually found my room along that I believe it must have been the very same, though I did walk a long time that night through long, long corridors before I could lie down.

I saw her the next morning in the hotel dining room. We happened to be queuing together, her behind me, while I waited for the chef to make my omelette (ham and cheese; I didn't hear what she ordered). The chef had run out of some ingredient and stood scratching at the grill with his spatula while a gray-haired waiter sped through the swinging doors at the back of the room. She was not very talkative. Having spent the rest of the day in bed (I had been feeling particularly prostrate), I saw her again that night at our usual table by the window in the bar. It was clear she had spent her time thinking of him. Her speech was fragmented by gaps and pauses where she seemed wholly unaware of my presence. In the brief time we had spoken together, what must have been three evenings by this stage (I must check this, but really, no, it is not important; the evenings we spoke together tend, when I think of them, to feel like one long unbroken night, and that is how it should be), I had learned to keep a book with me, as she would often lapse into silence for long periods. I thought it strange that she never brought his research down for me to look over, not even a photo of a sink-hole (those descriptions did intrigue me), despite my asking at least twice, and considering she was so desperate to find him. If she had, I would gladly have spent some time examining these abandoned documents and reading his work, the exact nature of which she never mentioned. Not having seen any paper beyond those two strange pages I have previously described, it was as if she were asking me to complete a jigsaw, the centre pieces of which she would not reveal, leaving an abyss of uncertainty (I stole this from Marcel Proust, whom I have recently been reading; it describes exactly my experience) whenever I sought an image of her brother in my mind. Eventually she returned to the circumstances of her brother in the hotel, recounting details I had heard previously, correcting small errors of memory in her narrative, which I would not have noticed had she not pointed them out, before returning, finally, to where she had left me on the previous night.

He had dug a hole in a field on the outskirts of the town. "It's obvious," she said, when I must have shown surprise (a raised eyebrow, maybe two). "It is not just a hole, but a pit, one so deep light cannot reach the bottom of it," she said. I didn't say it at the time, but of course light couldn't get inside, how could it when shadows are holes themselves. Shadows and pits must be kin: I saw this especially in those winter evenings when the shadows seemed to grow around her as she spoke, growing in their dark intensity whenever she spoke directly about sinkholes and pits, retreating when she returned to the life of her brother, his deter-mined character. "If you hadn't known he was down there, you would believe the pit to be an act of nature," she said. A sinkhole, opened by Chaak, perhaps, that god who is one and many, I thought, perhaps that god had possessed her brother, in order to open that earth beneath that field. But rarely are sinkholes bot-tomless, she had said. I thought it best to make sure, once again, that she wasn't chasing her brother down a rabbit hole of her own making: "Do you think he wanted this phrase to be true, knowing that if it were, he would be lost inside that phrase, that pit, I mean?" I asked. Without hesitating, she said: "Who would not want to believe that truth can exist in this world—I want to make this clear: my brother did not stumble." Her lips trembled. She reached for her glass. Raising it, she paused, then slowly placed it back on the white paper mat. Her tongue explored the dip in the centre of her upper lip, then swept across each side. She reached into her handbag, removed a stick of lipstick, and carefully traced a red, which complimented the dark of her eyes, over her upper, then lower, lip so that when she next took a sip of her drink, an imperfect red print remained below the rim of her glass.

She told me that the farmer who owned the field had warned her that it would have to be filled in, that his sheep could fall inside if it were left. "And my poor brother down there, stuck there in all of its falsity; how he must hate it," she said. "And to have sheep falling down on top of him!" Her eyes became suspiciously dewy. My question, I saw, had not helped. I quickly suggested the pit might be bottomless, that maybe he had dug through to some sort of void, and there found his truth, that he was happy—I couldn't finish the sentence; the idea of anyone finding any sort of happiness as they plunge through something like that, a continual leaving, a returning. The longer one falls, the greater the distance from that last step. The feeling of falling must become familiar, and the idea of returning to earth and solidity again must become very strange. I wondered if he dreamt as he fell, and did he dream of walking on the earth again, as others dream of flying? She left early that night, saying she had a headache. I stayed on, drinking steadily, my eyes too strained to read, blinking, watching the sleet falling under a street lamp outside. I much prefer snow to sleet, and sleet to rain. I like to see the evidence of it having fallen, and I suppose this comes from my childhood, when snow would mostly disappear on touching the ground, despite my wishing it to stay and build into a white carpet.

The next evening, I arrived in the bar early, as I wanted to finish the book I had been reading so I could begin another with the title *The Tartar Steppe*. It was odd, when I think of it, to have found those books there among the thrillers and romances. Buzzati's work has barely been translated into English; and what has is usually sold by rare bookshops, and often for hundreds of euro online. Yet I have memories of reading works of his that have not yet been translated, *The Secret of the Old Woods*, for example, but I did read them, sitting there in an overstuffed armchair, pleasant piano music mingling with pleasant thoughts of her, and her brother, though the more I attempted to picture him, the greater was the emptiness which grew over that faint outline, and even this was quickly supplanted by images of her, and whatever else happened to stride out from the darkness of my mind. I did not reach the steppe of the title that evening, did not even leave the protagonist's home, thanks to the particularly chatty, and forceful, waiter. Our conversation fell to the woman: I had resisted; but he had pushed. She had become well known in the small village (of which the hotel, with its long history, was the main tourist attraction), the waiter told me. People sympathised with her brother's task. I suggested it was a bit idealistic, a bit quixotic to put your life at risk just so you could write two words; did people not find it silly? He didn't seem to understand why anyone would. He asked me if I had ever thought of digging my own pit. He was very insistent that this was a normal thing to do, and that everyone should test the structure of their lives, that people in the village were always digging, that it was a fact of life out there. I told him I was not built for work like that. When I asked if he had seen the hole himself, he said he was far too busy; not being a dilettante, he had to work for a living, and, as if to illustrate this, he snatched my barely empty glass away and marched to the room behind the bar, bending his head to go through the little door. As he walked away, I saw his contorted features reflected in the mirror above the bar. He looked pale, though it was difficult to tell in the low light. Sensing movement by the edge of my vision, I turned to glance out the window and, having missed whatever it was, saw my own reflection, pale and frightened. There is no need to be frightened, I said to my reflection. And my reflection told me there was no need to be pale. We drank to that, to our agreement. (And now I drink to this, this memory of a rare harmony.)

Some time later that night I woke to find her sitting next to me, her hands resting in the lap of her dress—two glasses beautifully filled on the table between us. Before I had even taken my first drink, she continued from where she had left off, telling me that while most people she had spoken to sympathised with her situation, nobody had wanted to go after her brother into the pit. They wouldn't go with her to the field. Not even the farmer who owned it. The waiter slept in an armchair near us, snoring like a dog. I suspected he was pretending to sleep so he could hear her story. But I was not about to try to stop her to spite him, though I would have liked to. At one point, when she was silent—alone in that field again—I scooped an ice cube from

my glass and flung it at him. And missed. People were afraid
of what might be down in the pit, they were afraid of where it
might lead to, she said. "They act like forever is a place you go
to," as she said this she caught herself. An abyss she had heard it
called. The underworld. They may not be Mayans but they are
humans. Many in the village wanted the pit filled, and concreted
over, though the farmer wanted it only filled—it being necessary
to his livelihood that the grass remain. A meeting in the church
hall on the topic of what to do had descended into shouting. She
had argued that the pit would only be filled in when her brother
had been found, or it would be filled in over her living body. The
district judge spoke up and agreed to help. Since nobody, including himself or the lone policeman of the village, wanted to go
near the pit, it was decided to use a criminal, a burglar, who had
recently been arrested. There were those who argued that if the pit
was bottomless, placing the criminal there would be tantamount
to letting him go free, others argued that there are degrees of freedom and being forced to live the rest of one's life in a perpetual
fall must be one of the least desirable freedoms imaginable. The
judge had remained steady in his sentencing, adding only that
it was a fitting punishment: "What goes up must come down,"
he had said with a smirk.

The judge gave the criminal the choice of prison or pit. The
criminal chose the pit.

We were interrupted by the entrance of the barman from
behind that little door behind the bar. A memory from earlier
in the day came back to me, one of a wasp, evidentially lost in
the winter, crawling sluggishly across my pillow, this dark little
remnant of summer on my white bed. I had discovered it on
my return from breakfast and, not wanting to kill it, slid a sheet
of paper beneath it, carried it over to the open window, and
dropped it onto the outside sill—that is what I had meant to
do, but a gust of wind carried the wasp beyond the sill where it
fell away. I might as well have squashed it.

She told me how she had gone to the field along with the
judge, an imperiously large man, the policeman who guarded the
criminal—dressed in jeans and a thick jumper, his hands cuffed

in front of him so that, she told me, from a distance he appeared
to have accepted his fate—the criminal's girlfriend, who stood a
little away from the criminal, and mostly looked at her phone,
the farmer who owned the field, and who had barely spoken to
her, and a young and nervous-seeming priest. Nobody would
step on to the grass. When the criminal hesitated; the policeman
had kicked him in his backside, sending him stumbling into the
field. She followed. The pit is in the middle of it, she reminded
me, a few minutes' walk from the roadside. Apparently, being
unable to find a tractor or crane, or anything of that sort, in
the country of all places, the farmer had rigged up his jeep with
a rope which was tied to the criminal who would be lowered
down. The wind carried the smell of burning leaves, and when
she looked back, she saw the priest and the girlfriend bless themselves, and the policeman position himself beside the coil, a long
scythe in his hand, its blade a sharp and archaic shadow in the
morning light. I interrupted to ask why the scythe. She said it
was to cut the rope if any problem arose. "Yes, but a scythe?"
"Yes, a scythe," she said, and as she did I thought I heard a hint
of an accent similar to that of the locals. It was only when she
and the criminal reached the edge that the criminal spoke, asking
if it was really bottomless. She couldn't remember what it was
she said to him, or, as I suspected, felt ashamed to reveal it, but
whatever it was made his face crumple, in a way that reminded
her of her brother, who, when he was younger, had a tendency
to cry at any and every provocation. By the time the farmer had
again parked beside the small crowd on the edge of the field the
rope was still taut. The criminal could not be seen in the deep
darkness below. There was some discussion among the small gathering which she couldn't hear, then the farmer shouted over that
he had reversed from four miles away. As he said this, the rope
fell slack. She shouted down asking the criminal if he had found
her brother. There was no reply. She pulled on the rope while the
others rushed over. The end of it, when it came to her, was cut
through, as if it were chopped, she said. The policeman sniffed
at it, but wouldn't say what it smelled like when the priest asked.

While they stood, a large black-feathered bird flew up from

the interior of the pit and toward them. Everyone gasped, with one or two (the priest and policeman) stumbling and falling backward as the bird skimmed low over their heads. The judge tutted, and said it was probably a bat. She grabbed at his elbow, pleading with him to do something. He brushed her hand away, and, after removing a piece of chewing gum from within his coat, and placing it on his outstretched tongue, told her that there was nothing to be done, apart from sending someone else down. "And that, madam, was my only criminal," he said. "I suppose they have to be heartless, don't they," she said. I nodded.

The girlfriend later told her about another pit that had been dug in another field a few months before, a few short minutes' walk from the one that had taken the two men: her brother, and her boyfriend. Apparently a man had dug it, one foreign to the village. While the girlfriend had not seen this pit, a friend of hers, a farm labourer, had. He had told her that whenever any-one shouted down to the man, who had dug himself so deep he could not be seen, that whenever they said anything, he replied saying: "It is a matter of justice." Many suspected there was nobody in that pit. People said how strange it was that the man would only say these words, and the labourer himself had won-dered if there was anyone down there, as the words, when the unseen man spoke, came up slowly, as if from the soil. The labourer had wondered if it was only an echo buried in the soil, unleashed by shouts from the surface. The memory of someone who once dug this deep hole separated from that person, lost in the soil like a piece of jewellery, shining there among the dirt.

In the course of our conversations, I gradually learned that, while I did my best not to step outside the hotel in all my time there, she, on the other hand, spent her mornings in that first field, sitting by the edge of the pit that might be bottomless, with its silent occupants, talking, sometimes, to those men down there, but mostly just thinking. And in the afternoons she would go looking for the other pit—searching the nearby fields for the man who still digs—before returning to the hotel for the last dinner setting, late in the evening, and to meet me in the bar afterwards. She was indefatigable. My conversations were a great relief for her (naturally), as was my advice, she told me. All this activity of hers made me feel guilty; I asked the waiter if he had ever seen her out of the hotel, and he confirmed that, yes, he would see her in the field in the mornings as he cycled home after his shift. Only her head could be seen, the rest of her being wrapped in the early morning mist. He suspected she had liqueur on her, and that kept the cold from digging too deep inside her body.

On the last night I sat with her, both of us were on the brandy. An elderly couple played chess on the other side of the room (he occasionally murmuring that it would be okay, and not to worry) while the waiter, and a waitress I had never seen before, discussed the returning to college of one or the other in their obnoxiously loud voices. Snow clumped against the window behind us. She had been telling me about the previous night when, lying in bed waiting for sleep, she had thought of a chapel she had visited while in Rome a few years ago. The altar was constructed from the bones of past monks, and the walls were covered, effusively decorated, with more of these bones, which might have belonged to animals, if it were not for the inclusion of the unmistakable humanity of the skulls. It was dark by the time she arrived at the chapel, and mist had filled the streets, obscuring much of the scenery she had hoped to enjoy. The chapel was lit by candles, the light livening the eyes of the skulls; making bones jump against the walls. She was sure she heard whispering, though she was alone. And remembering it then, in the dark of her hotel room, with the distant sounds of guests or hotel workers making a clanging noise somewhere, she heard the whispering as that of her brother: Chaak is one, Chaak is many. She dragged her hands over her ears, and continued pressing down to her neck, reaching her hands below, clasping the back of her head, feeling for the bone beneath the skin—she broke off and, as if an idea had suddenly come to her, said, "I'm very sorry, but I have to leave. It was lovely to talk with you, really it was." As she stood up, her arm glanced against her glass. It teetered, then settled loudly on the table.

As I drank my orange juice at the breakfast table the next morning, the waiter arrived, poured more coffee, leered, and made a remark about a lovers' tiff. I did not reply. He was forced to elaborate to the effect that the woman had checked out of the hotel in an agitated state soon after leaving me in the bar the previous night. I did not believe him, knowing something of his character, I knew to distrust anything that waiter said. However, I also knew, somehow, that she had indeed left, that we would not be meeting that evening, and I felt a relief on not having to listen to her: I could read in peace; but this was coupled with a feeling of incompleteness. She had left without bothering to say goodbye. Had it been out of embarrassment at telling me so much about her brother, and her fears for him, the dream of that last night being the ultimate in self-revelation? I have often felt something similar to this in the aftermath of having been too free with others, of having opened up those layers closest to myself to another, a fear that I have given something that should not be given. If this was why she left like that I do not blame her.

I realised I had grown to like this brother of hers, what I knew of him—which was little. If I knew any more it is probable I would find something in him to hate, in fact I am certain I would, and conversely I am sure I would find something in him to like, and so on, and so on, until, theoretically, I would know everything there is to know about him, but I have never known anyone that much. Yes, it was precisely because I barely knew him that I could so easily like him. I considered going outside and searching for him, or her, for both of them; I felt strongly that if I were to find one I would find the other. Perhaps it was out of sympathy, having lost a brother of my own when I was younger, or it might have been a determination to resolve this story she had been telling me, to get to the bottom of this bottomless pit, so to speak, which now as I write it I see is an impossible task, much as he must have known it would be, but, as I say, the exact reason why I considered leaving the hotel evaded me. Through the window the landscape, usually intolerable enough with its hills and forests, slopes and short walls and solitudinous houses built and lived in by solitary families, and always with a rusting barn not too far off so that everywhere looked like everywhere else and nothing stood apart: all of this was covered in snow, smothered in the stuff. I anticipated the silence of it, and the breaking of that silence when my shoe would first plunge through that white surface. At the table next to me the elderly couple were whispering, concerned, I assumed, that I was listening to their conversation; I was, but they managed to speak very quietly. Finishing my coffee, I went to the library in the bar, chose a new Buzzati—one I had been most looking forward to—and went back to bed.

Relic

THERE IS A VAULT DEEP beneath the Vatican which is said to be as large as the city of Rome, if not larger; every day our workers excavate its walls in every direction. Despite the heat, this must be done with special care. That cavern, for it was once a natural cavern, just barely contains a fragment of skin thought to be the last surviving remnant of the first pope. Scholars compete to tell the true story. Many believe this skin once wrapped a bone from that pope's thumb, others believe it housed his nose: a regal Roman one. I am inclined to believe the latter.

The skin has grown without pause since his death, apparently. It is folded and layered upon an antiquated system of brass poles, pipes, and pulleys. The skin is so entwined within this system, which nobody has yet to fully understand, that the system cannot be dismantled to make way for a new and efficient mechanism. A team of workers maintain the old materials as best they can. Many have fallen from the upper layers of piping and, afraid to break their fall with that skin, drop freely to the subterranean earth, which might only paralyse them. Most die. Yet, some have landed on the skin and, grinning wildly, slid down to the earth, happy to climb back up to their interrupted work once the supervisor allowed it, once the doctor—my wife— has asserted, yes, the bones seem fine, the skin unblemished. Another team polishes the apparatus daily to avoid the terror of snagging that holy skin. This, I believe, is the Church's greatest worry.

If the skin were to be placed flat on the ground it might cover the continent of Eurasia, which is not very impressive; I once read that the intestines of any person, like me for instance, if I could somehow live and at the same time spread them flat on the ground, would stretch for 50,000 miles . . . Now that I put it on paper, I think it might in fact be my circulatory system, my blood vessels or something, but still the idea stands: this saint's skin was not so impressive to my mind.

Just recently, in its unending struggle to contain the skin, the Vatican has begun to dig downward. There are fears of what might be found—if the earth's molten core were to erupt inside that chamber, the church might fall and the skin disintegrate, for who knows how strong this old skin might be. Although, it may only be the earliest parts of the fragment that are so old, other sections—for example, that square metre which grew this month—they could be said to be newly born while remaining a part of this first pope, just as the endings of the uppermost branches of a tree are called buds—those blind tips that look so distinctly newborn, the progeny of those first roots. And yet, the new skin looks very much like the old skin. I often wonder if it ages like us, or does it simply grow. And when I think this, when I fall into this thought, I quickly lose the distinction between those two things, through the nulling effect of repetition, perhaps, or I am falling further from things that I know and closer to the unknown and, as happens in these moments, I must reach out for another topic—to avoid . . . I don't know exactly, knowing? truth?

It is the task of one man to make the daily measurement. As the skin might grow in any direction, or might spread its minuscule growth throughout its manifold edges so that to a stranger no growth would appear to have taken place, his job requires patience and expertise. He is old, and often supported by a harness affixed to another system of rigging reportedly designed by one of the better-known minds of the Renaissance. (Inventors spread like lice then, but, I am glad to say, they are no longer a problem.) The rigging covers the vast roof of the cavern. It was constructed with the aim of manoeuvring such a person over every segment, every ridge, pimple, and callus so that he might measure the progress of the whole. He writes down nothing,

and never speaks to us. He caresses the skin so gently. He must
dream of the skin. It must be a part of him: I am surprised he
leaves it, to go where, I don't know, but he goes, each night, like
the rest of us. I cannot imagine the skin of the ordinary person
sufficing for him who gets to caress that vast living sheet each
day. I like to watch him as he works. In fact, this is how I discovered the conversations he has with the skin. Of course they
are too mumbled on either side for me to hear, that is if there
are two sides to this conversation. He may put on a voice for the
skin as some do with their pets, or that first pope might indeed
speak to him, ask him the latest about his football team, about
the weather on the surface.

The doctor, my wife, tells me the old man is losing it, that
she has done tests which say as much. She believes only what her
instruments tell her. That is why I will never let her know about
the strange vertigo that so often strikes me when I wake. It is not
the type poor Jimmy Stewart suffered in Hitchcock's film, but
one more temporal: a confusion of time. The past, just four years
ago—a time when I did not yet know my wife—invariably feels
more real to me than this present, and I hate that I feel this way,
but I do. In that time I lived alone, spoke very little, and worked
even less: I was despair itself. And it lasted for much longer than
how I have been living most recently. How backwards it feels:
each morning, moments after waking I believe I am still in that
time, and must force myself to remember my current life, my
wife, this smooth happiness. How strange to have to tug this
reality out from under my pillow each morning only to tuck it
away each night.

My wife could surely tell me why I crawl back to unhappi-
ness each night. But I could never let her know. I don't even
know how I would react if she revealed she felt the same way.
Perhaps I would feel relieved; we would be equal then. Maybe
everyone who works with the skin feels the same way, or indeed
it has nothing to do with the skin but is something universal
which nobody dares reveal for fear of that revelation revealing
something deeply different to the experiences of everyone else,
that it would expose our darkest sediment: a place where only

Dante and his poet could return from. Still, I can't help but wonder how she would react. If I were to tell her and she were to understand, would she attempt to treat me, or would she be content with being my wife, would she first reach for me with her warm arms, or would it be her stethoscope that I feel cold against my chest?

On a particularly hot day in late summer, a friend of mine fell dead. He was typical in that he would not even look at the skin as he fell—more a colleague, really. I took the opportunity to stay back when everyone else went home, saying I would do his work that evening, that this would be a sort of tribute, and more importantly, that if he could not do his work, someone must: the skin does not stop so we cannot stop, and so on. I think they were grateful. Once alone in that echoing cavern, I felt afraid, and thought of leaving, and catching up with my friends who would be drinking by that time, but I did not leave. I touched the skin. It felt so warm. I wrapped myself in that skin and held my ear to its deep surface.

I cried for the first time I can remember since losing my mother. I cried tears that soaked my shirt collar, cried and cried, whole rivers and lakes formed in the skin around me. I was an island of my own making. The skin was so warm and comfortable, so forgiving, it seemed.

Sometime round about midnight I remembered myself, stood up, and with as much care as I could manage, unfolded and placed that part of the skin back the way it belonged, in the way I knew by heart from seeing it each morning. I went home and watched my sleeping wife. I do love her. I carefully placed the sheet that had fallen on the floor back over her pale body, and lay beside her. And my breathing slowed to where we became one person, and rather than becoming overly conscious of this and waking a little more, I felt very light—floating, almost.

In work the next day, the man who measured the skin was pronounced dead. They refused to reveal the cause of his death or the location of the body, and it seemed everyone felt that this was a great mystery, that this was something worth discussing, something that demanded their understanding. I would like to say I felt the same. In fact, my wife did, and I had to feign illness (not an easy thing to do with a doctor for a spouse) to escape her theories on the whereabouts of his poor body, the cause of his death, and the possible effects of the skin on the former. I feel the same when people go on about the wonder of that first pope's still-living skin. It is no more wondrous than the fact that I exist, that somewhere inside my own skin there is an I which contains all of my history yet continues to be I, that my wife (is it too late to introduce her? no? Sylvia, beautiful name isn't it?), that Sylvia—another mystery bound in soft skin—and I found each other and, despite our vast differences, live together. And that every now and then, we find some happiness. There is no understanding any of this, but does that not merit even a little attention, a little discussion?

*

It does not, it seems; I write it down instead, and must be content with that, just as I must leave now to go measure the skin in my new position—I have become the official measurer, exciting isn't it.

It all happened very fast, but everyone says I am growing more and more suited to my new role. The skin has also grown—a total of twelve feet over the past month, a record for this, albeit short, century, and most of that time it has lain unmeasured while our superiors deliberated as to who could resume the measuring. Everything has changed so quickly since that poor man's death. For example, since my new position at work I no longer wake as if I had not yet met Sylvia. I guess that feeling was just a remnant from my dreams. Perhaps our dreams, like Achilles, must travel farther to catch up with our lived life, which—though much slower than the life of dreams—is, like the tortoise from Zeno's paradox, always just ahead. We must live before we dream. It must be a rule of nature, the way shadows can never overtake the light.

Whatever it is, my dreams have changed. Last night, I dreamt that the cavern had caved in and I was the only one inside. The skin wrapped itself around me until I ran out of air. This was a slight variation on the dream of the previous night, which varied slightly again from the previous night's dream, and so on. I have to write these down, just as my predecessor did. I am not allowed to see his writings; and I am not sure I want to either. Our dreams hold the key to the future of the skin, apparently.

The having, and subsequent recording, of these dreams are an unwelcome aspect of the job, but it pays so much better than my last position. Sylvia and I are even looking to buy a house— somewhere close to our shared work. When I wake now, I open my eyes expecting to see her, and I am very glad of that, but the idea of our work and the skin is incomprehensible to me in those moments, the idea that I measure it, touch it. How strange.

Fog

IF I BREATHE THE FOG I wheeze and lose my breath. I wear a scarf then, around my nose and mouth. I breathe through the scarf and steam my glasses. I lower the scarf and the fog clouds my chest. I raise the scarf and become blind. I remain blind. Nothing is clear. All is covered; it cannot always have been like this, always unknowable. I surely remember surfaces. Is it only through the fog that reality makes itself known: something that cannot be seen, that does not exist unless disguised? People emerge, walking on this path, and I cannot see their faces. They must think I am producing the fog somehow, why else would it rest between my glasses and eyes if I were not a friend (or more than that). Beneath a streetlamp, a red truck curves through the fog, just the front of it. It is fat and placeless, the yellow light revealing gray cloud more than anything real. I am sure it is carried by the fog. No truck has ever existed, ever looked like that. The fog disarranges, it takes.

It is in my house and I do not know until the morning because the fog did something to the electricity, bit the wires, weighed down on the wires, I don't know. I wear my scarf inside and, compromising slightly, have removed my glasses. The fog has reduced me to my natural blindness. It has acknowledged this in subtle ways that are too slight, or too old, to be labelled. There is no definition for what the fog has done. I can only talk round it using words formed for other purposes, and even then . . .

I can say that things are not where they used to be, and it is not because I am blind now, or because the fog has covered everything in that damp grasp. It does grasp: when I woke this morning my scarf was lying on the floor by the window and the fog was squeezing my chest. It blew away when I opened my eyes—not too far away, just by the bed's end, leering. Walls move in the night. Floors collide when I walk. The radio is muffled, no matter how loud the volume goes, it is only audible up close, ear held to the soft speaker. The things that made my home have been rearranged for a stranger. I no longer feel at home. It is as if the fog were preparing for my departure, the date of which is known only to it. Yet among that gray spread I see nothing to know with, it cannot know anything, at least in the way I am used to. If I am to understand this fog, I must change my thinking, I must unthink, I must drift.

The fog is in the house, wandering through these old corridors, seeping beneath the doors I shut behind me, creeping through the thick walls. There are passageways in those walls: I was told about them as a child but have never found an entrance. I know the fog knows those secrets, and it doesn't care; there are no feelings in that fallen cloud. And it is all in this old house. The outside is clear and bright now. I feel that original light only when I press against the windows. It feels so cold despite the sun and I realise it must be the fog's many shoulders bunched against the glass: barricading this gloom—I mean room. From where does the fog gather its shoulders? Is this why it lingers in cemeteries at night?

I fear I am losing myself: I confuse the cul-de-sacs of my body for its motorways, no, the roundabouts of my body for its promenades . . . I confuse myself in ways I cannot imagine, and that is the most uncomfortable thing, more so than the pervading damp, the loss of sight: it is the disordering I cannot live with. The other day I was drinking and expected an umbrella by the door to lift the cup. I thought that umbrella was my arm! despite it leaning against a wall almost seven feet from where I sat. But it might have been. Distances were once so ordered, but now, it is easy for them to change beneath the fog. I know it gloats when I lose myself like this. These thoughts I have are just one of its many ways of gloating. For example, I expect a woman to enter the room in this next moment. In each succeeding moment, I expect she will walk through the door. I don't know her, and I have not been in a relationship in at least a year. Her identity is blank to me. It taunts me. I could wear earmuffs to keep it out, but then my eyes, my nose, this mouth—my skull is too open.

Closing the windows at night. These ancient rugs, these once-polished floorboards, they squelch underfoot. I look down and see they have been replaced by gray mud. It is tiresome to walk. I keep tripping over what feel like limbs—hard and slightly forgiving—but I do not look down: I am afraid. I cannot stop my ears and so I hear the distant cries and hollow booms of what must have been artillery.

I put the house up for sale. I explain thoroughly the symptoms of the house, the presence of the fog, what it does to you, etc. I would not like to force the fog on another, especially not an innocent, and most likely not even on someone considered evil. It must be their decision. A man arrives. I ask, "Are you sure, did you read what I wrote about the fog?" (and all that). I myself had become unsure about whether this was the right thing to do, whether I had chosen the correct course to follow (it is so difficult in this setting). He says, "I have, of course, I read everything you wrote."

He is excited. He says he has a special interest in this form of weather. I say—I can't remember what I say—but I am surprised by his not mentioning the word—*fog*—we have been speaking in the kitchen for at least an hour, all about the *fog*, and yet he says everything he can in order to avoid saying *fog*. He speaks round and round it, his conversation winding inward until words finally brush against that one word in the centre, that word which stands for what surrounds us, even in this cold room, that word I find myself saying so often, that I cannot stop thinking: *fog*. As he speaks closer to the word, he shivers and his eyes, his pupils, they shiver, too. This is irritating to me: if he does not want to mention it, he must be in denial, he must simply want the house for its location, the low price, the transport links, each of which is very good. I ask him, "Why do you not call it what it is, say it, *fog*, say it with me, *fog fog fog*.

Fog! Here it is." I snatch at the *fog*. Almost violently he pulls my outstretched arm toward him and wrenches my fingers open. He laughs, or blushes (I am not sure; the fog is between us), and he says, "I am very sorry, but you should not do that." His hands are cold, clammy.

He cannot accept or understand that I do not want the fog, that I am unhappy that the fog will not move on, that it seems to have rooted itself in my things. It is as if he suspects I am teasing him with the promise of a house of fog. The house has been changed but he resists it. (The way he names it, as if *he* were the parent!) "I have read about this happening centuries ago. There was a time it occupied a whole village in Japan, but that was doubly rare. This is such an opportunity, and to think, I am here now." He denies it despite it already being inside him. I do see it there, in his eyes, wisping from his lips. No matter, he is naive— if he refuses, so be it. He cannot. He advised me to move into a smaller home. I said, "You could try living somewhere smaller," or he did. "I will move into a small apartment." I am sure I said this. "The smaller the square footage the less likely this weather is to be comfortable, it likes to spread out, you see; you were very lucky to have it move in with you. I have spent much of my life chasing it. Some countries are blessed, the northern ones, those cold, dark lands, others, those in southern Europe for example, they are too hot, to dry for it to breathe. That air chokes it." He repeats himself: "Chokes it." He appears aghast—the fog drifts apart so I can see this.

This house I had lived in had belonged to my grandfather. A house built in another century. A house that deigned to accommodate people. It could have been built for fog, those cold rooms with their high ceilings, those endless corridors, with so many corners, and doors—half of which I am sure I have never been through, their keys having been lost so many years ago. A house of fog. I am glad to leave it to that pale man. Watery is the word, he is a watery man, as my grandmother would say. A man born of fog, or married to it, I would say. I am glad to leave, and yet nobody can be fully glad to leave a place, no matter how awful it has been. (I have heard of incarcerated men who on leaving their cells for the last time, turn back: they capture that small room with a long stare, to keep with them for the days ahead, those days of what others call freedom.) There are parts of you that remain, memories that can only be remembered by walking through that room, or when the leaves of the apple trees can be seen from the landing's front window, as you pass into the library, prompting the remembering of an especially enjoyable evening. All those memories might wither when left in that house that has become so estranged.

"The fog is a low-lying creature," he told me. My new apartment is very high, not at the top of this building, but close. I recently saw a girl fall past the window. She wore a modest, inexpensive spring dress bought off the rack. She looked very calm. She was waving to the floor above me as she passed by: that is how high I live now—she was so far from her destination that it had not yet seemed in any way problematic to her.

Winter arrives. I watch the fog crawl in from the sea, and make sure to shut all the doors and windows. It rises up from the sea, an ancient thing. I watch it swallow the city, and soon there is nothing but a thin line of sky between the gray fog and the gray clouds above it. If I were not indoors, in this room with its clean air, I would lose my balance, and not know where to stand, but I am, and do, I think.

The winter passes and I believe I have escaped the fog's tendrils, and I did, in a way. My apartment is empty, blissfully so, but still, empty. There is no fog, and more than that, there are no memories. I cannot remember. Almost all of my base memories begin within that house, and without its surroundings to call them forth, I am lost in the present, which is a fine place to visit, but I cannot survive without all that I have lived through. In this apartment I am perpetually born. I decide I will go back, just to remember, just for a while.

His voice has no accent—had I not recognised that before? The words he speaks pass through his mouth as if it were only a corridor they must file through. His face has become smooth: young and old at once, the features average, horribly average. His suit shines with hardened dirt. I see the fog in his face. How does he not see it cloud his eyes, does he never look in the mirror? It slowly works on him. Why else would he return? Not for me. I am no longer me. I am a vessel. Nobody could want or desire this presence in any way, and if they suppose they do, it is the mystery they desire, not what was once me. I am the memory of being. A great cloud. This fallen cloud.

"I have come to remember, that's all," I said, warning him, in effect, that I would not want to chat, to sit around with cups of tea and coffee in our kitchen like I once used to do so often (he does talk, and how!). I walk through the house, searching for those sensations that will rush me back to where I would like to be, just for a moment, or however long the memory might last. I linger on the staircase, midway down, where I can see the door, but I cannot see the door. I see fog. If I am to recognise anything I must peer right up next to it, so that my face rubs its surface. And then I am in the wrong position to remember—never before had I to peer like this. I see a woman, always the back of her as she leaves the room. Every room I enter she leaves by a different door. The hem of her long skirt, the line of her calf, the heel of her shoe, the closed door. She reminds me of other women. She is every woman, might as well be, since I cannot see her face, her hands. But I have seen her before, earlier, when?

The woman and the surfaces: that is all this house is to me. And this man that now owns what was once my home: this man and fog. I believe that were I to touch him—to touch his elbow to guide him through the doorway with the palm of my hand—his elbow would burst and my hand would go right through, I believe my palm would come away wet and smelling of the nearby lake. I think and believe this and cannot fathom why.

The long groan of a ship's horn sounds muffled in the distance of the landing, and through the fog, I see a light, waving slowly from side to side, brightening, darkening the gray fog. He says that woman I keep missing is a woman who has taken to living here. An artist. I want to not see him and ask if I could retrieve something personal from what was once my bedroom. He is happy to let me go. He is slowly wrapped in oblivion. I realise I have forgotten my scarf. Left it at home. Or he breathes oblivion. The air is thick with cold. A voice. I turn onto the stairs.

These stairs won't end. I keep climbing into this graying . . . My legs never tiring, my breath abundant, as if it were not coming from inside me but from some great bank of breath. I turn the corner and continue climbing, past the wall hangings, the portraits, not even touching the bannister. My legs run ahead of me. It was he who lived here. I arrive and see the mirror—see that which is reflected: that face that is clouded, beneath it the shirt and neck, but this face . . .

*

Billowing slightly, it settles over the two men and the woman who sit at the long table. They are the dull lighthouse, the broken mast, the cliff: painted by an old master. They are wrapped in that low cloud. They are barely there.

A Tourist

1.

THERE IS EVERY POSSIBILITY I passed by here one time, on my way somewhere I rarely go (a funeral, a meeting, perhaps a picnic), and with one sideward glance marked this landscape as a place where there must be loss; it is a ruin you see. Ruins are the bones of loss, and grief, that is in there, too, trapped inside the crevices, beneath the having fallen. It was here, among the more discernible of nature's ruins, that I am sure I once was. I was, I am sure of it, before the destruction, when everything was as it should be. And I lost something here. In those scattered rocks, or that cleaved cliff face? In the air of this valley? It is here, and there must be an investigation because no matter how hard I try, I cannot find any remembrance of this loss. There is only that certainty. Laughable, really. So foolish these days to think and act like this: a bloodied animal on the side of the road, that's how others would see me if they were to look. They cannot see me here in this valley; it is large, but not unimaginably so. I will mourn the savage ruination from within these bounds.

What cowardness: a tourist visiting a grief unanchored to any being. Great monuments of grief just waiting for my acknowledgment, waiting to pose for my flattened photograph while I crouch behind a camera, shoulders jutting forward around my innards, a stable base from which to shoot. They can wait for all time, and have done.

Should I leave then? I should, by any account I should leave

immediately—but I would not write my experiences in these
pages then. I should leave, and tell myself, yes, I will diary my
living and when I am gone that will be remembered, and provide a structure, a frame for the memories others must hold of
me. This is the purpose of diaries, no? look at what I thought,
and did, "How long I stuck with that breakfast cereal." "Why
not Black and White *and Gray*?" "How my left knee ached this
evening, I should probably see the doctor."

But that is morbid and boring and anyway there is no need
to face that because I am stupid, or stubborn, or whatever lies
in that minuscule space between the two, because I am staying.
Yes, I am staying, so I will have something to record, to demon-
strate my brave extraction from the usual, dulling, trudging. To
highlight myself for even a short while. Yes, how *brave* of me.

Now look at it. Not even the sloping sides of the valley grow
green: no trees, no bushes, it is perfect. This is a landscape that
actively swallows the things of civilisation, the things that must
be valued. This is a place where the breath of life has been buried
and this is where I will find grief, and bury that, too. I know this.

There is another possibility, and this is one I prefer not to
believe: I am acting. I am acting a role to be read. Replace and
rearrange one or two letters and these pages become a stage: get
it, stage, pages? There I go. I can't help but attempt to entertain,
even when I am my sole audience. If this is a role I believe I
should play for the benefit of myself, do I even need to remember what it is I lost? I could just pretend. I could just pretend to
pretend, just pretend to pretend to pretend, write it all down in
a coffee shop. This is a possibility that has no ending. Writing
that last sentence gives me vertigo complete with that strange
abdominal feeling (and it is not wind). There is no coping with
no ending, not for me, and I am quite usual. What exactly is
wrong with pretence?

2.

". . . not even ghosts, we are all that remains, there is nothing . . .
It's all inside you! You have to listen to me . . . ," he said.

"Enough! Come back in two weeks," I shouted. My driver
left muttering about spirits that have deserted this place, about
how only the foolish would try to live where even spirits cannot,
or something like that; the wind carried much of it away and
up the sides of the valley. If I were to listen to everything everyone has ever said to me, I would have no room left to listen to
myself, and then who would I be, a skin of sound? fit to burst
with everyone's opinion but my own. A mass of sound grown
quiet. How ugly.

I prepared my camp. Should have asked for his help, should
have said sorry, said, Yes I know this is no place for the living, but
that is exactly what I am looking for, almost exactly, should have
said: Despite my explaining it all, you obviously did not even
listen, so why am I even bothering to apologise, you should be
apologising to me, you know this is extremely important to me,
do you realise I have been searching for something like this my
whole life—this is my being born, have you ever been born, do
you even know what that feels like? so yes, you should apologise,
do it now or I will fire you right here in this, this valley, get on
your knees, yes I'm serious, I should have said that, but no, I had
to put up my tent myself. I heard it ripping but cannot find the
tear. It exists somewhere among this gray fabric.

3.

Here are the walls of the tent at night. The light of the propane
canister on the walls of the tent. The animals that do not exist:
they live beside me at night, and the fauna of the tropics, and
great machines that sprawl across the walls of my tent. Where
is that damn hole? I am not cold but it does unnerve the body,
even just the knowing of it.

4.

Who ever wants to hear about dreams. Not when they are posed next to pillows behind closed eyes. (There are performers who paint their eyelids with large inhuman eyes that open unseeing while the human eyes look inward.) To hide the origins of dreams: that is what must be done if knowledge is to be extracted, that is if there is anything in there (what do those human eyes see?). How is anyone to know unless they are parsed? I would trust Dr. Jung, but not Dr. Freud.

A young lady, on her way to an appointment with Jung, noticed a man sitting by a lake in the grounds of the asylum in which the doctor worked—the man was himself. Disbelieving her eyes, she continued to her appointment. On her arrival, Jung's secretary informed the young lady that Dr. Jung was busy. But, surely not, she said, I just saw him sitting by the lake outside, look—she pointed through the open window to where Jung could be seen lying on the grass. The secretary informed her that Dr. Jung had an appointment with himself today, would you like to reschedule? Miss . . . ?

5.

I slept through the hot day, and woke late to find the door of my tent flapping monotonously in the wind (nature bores into you). It was closed when I went to sleep. And now it is open. There is someone else in this valley. I should have known. Their presence echoes from every surface, has done since I first stepped out of the car—if only I had listened. But how could I have done so when I was being deafened by my driver's ranting. He is unbalanced, that man. Mad.

But this, the opening of my tent is an act of communication. How long has this person lived out here? They must perceive my presence as a threat. (How could they not?) Can they read? I could scatter notes outside, explaining my purpose, proving my innocence, my inability to harm. Rubbish. I keep doing it!

Believing I know myself, what do I know? Nothing! I scream out here. Even in those honest moments before sleep, I cannot find my own purpose, let alone that of a stranger. They could do anything, could be anyone, and I am myself. Here in this valley I am myself, here, where I am least sure what that means. (I like that. That's true.) I know that if I stayed here long enough the sun would crack me open, and I would see myself as I exist, and all the rest of it would fall away. This, now, I think I want this, it would be painful, sure, but I would discover the mounds of grief inside me and tear them free, plant them where they belong, inside this hard rock, this naked valley.

6.

There is my younger self striding into old age. Toward the camera, it seems. I tint the memory because of course it is old, and old things must be different in some way. Where does he go? I do not recognise those ruins. What is that expression? I take photographs of this old face and try to feel what I once felt by minute adjustments of my facial muscles. There is no returning. I look like an idiot and delete each one: goodbye, goodbye, goodbye.

(It has taken me half this day to map the width of the valley, but I did not commit the number to memory. I am tired now and hungry. Tomorrow I will map the farthest length. And I will forget that, too. I am losing myself. Yes, it is working. This is all true. I am becoming, yes.)

7.

I couldn't sleep, and thought about stories I had read, and attempted to balance their sentences in the dark so as to bring close to me those writers, who by the nature of their writing, must surely have known this raw existence. It is always in stories that I find what I need, but the effort! I have read so much and nothing has remained. Sure, a few words arrive together, and, holding them in one hand, I grasp about for what follows, that which flutters from reach. I stretch my hand and finally catch hold of one—say, *jasmine*—only to turn back to find my other hand empty again, not even *the* remaining . . . In the act I strengthened other memories. I saw a pair of hiking boots, brown, or mud splashed, perched on a rock. I was looking at them from the front, the toes pointing directly toward my face (or neck). I fell asleep with those lost words, those boots, my mute understanding. I am realising this is an exercise of memory. If exercised enough I could remember every memory borne by this valley, this drug, filling my veins with its gray basalt, these black boulders.

8.

I have searched for evidence of the other's presence: a lost boot, the remains of a camp, a worn trail, anything. I feel they can help me with this lost grief. I have exhausted both the valley and myself to the point I saw my family, whole generations of them, walk down from the mountains holding hands, calling to me, beckoning frantically from the very edge of the valley floor, and I in the very middle. I saw their faces, but they were so mysterious, so knowing, hidden.

It is flat down here, oh, if only I could write how flat and empty this land is. How the eye, or better, the sight, cannot follow the emptiness of the floor and must rush to the sides, to the slopes and up where grass grows and goats surely roam. But down here: nothing can prepare the mind for such desolation.

9.

Who would believe they might exist? the sheer audacity of it. You would do better believing yourself a tightrope walker than believe in that. I should have been driven away, and left what waits for me in the valley, for the elements to dispose with their, typical, slow fury. Things I do not like creep in this valley, they have no need for time, and must laugh at these eyes I wear. There is violence everywhere, always has been, but I feel it most frenzied in the stone that once filled this place. It has been frozen here since God knows. It has been waiting for someone to set it free. I would not unbound this land for fear of what it would make me. Fear and terror, the person and nature. What life I could carve from this stone, what evil.

Oh, this is a place of indecency, nature is not moral no matter the tiny bird's summer singing (and yet they are so delicate and beautiful). And I am a part of it all, inescapably so.

Too tired. Writing makes me jittery. Impatient—my arm is weak. I want to smash it against the ground. Crack each bone away from me.

10.

This morning I found a skull a few feet from my tent, facing down my approach to the path I take into the centre of the valley each day. A human skull, bereft of reason. Overwhelmed, I ran to my phone, where it lay charging on the roof of my tent by solar panel. I rang my driver. There was no reception, not that I was surprised. I sat inside the tent opening, to the side, a heavy torch in one hand, phone in the other—my fingers incessantly swiping—for what must have been hours. When night came, I did nothing. I must have fallen asleep like that.

I woke with the sun balanced above me. I placed the skull on a rock and sat across from it as I ate. The skull was expressionless: teeth and sun-tanned bone: a vision of a future which, though awful, must be peaceful at times, has to be, or else so many would surely return. I tried to see the face it once drew in muscle and flesh. I imagined it as the face of the hidden being in the valley, and this brought back to me an incident from last night:

I sensed a living presence and stepped outside of my tent. A bear or goat I had thought. It was not an animal but the other. Their face remained in darkness, despite my shining a torch in their direction. A fuzzy darkness like a photo of the night sky aggressively scratched. I was waiting for this, but I was not prepared. How can one prepare for this? Their hands drew figures, constellations, it seemed, and all I could do was nod and say things, none of which altered the intricate movement of those hands. Those hands had left the skull for me to find, that was obvious.

11.

Jealous of his best friend—the pampered Hamlet—and knowing of Hamlet's love for his murdered father, perhaps Horatio conjured the ghost of Hamlet's father by some trickery. There are clear signs all along the play, but no explanation of the workings of his magic, which suggests the author was unaware of his character's secret life. This is what I remember in this valley. Deception and revenge and grief wrapping the sorry lot in some deadman's bundle. Why not let the ghost be a ghost, since it is only a play, and so far from life in most ways. But I want it to be a trick. Something unseen by everyone—especially Shakespeare—a sly character hiding his true feelings, pretending to be so supportive, laughing at Hamlet's laboured jokes even toward the end, when really, he laughs at Hamlet's misfortune. If I could just remember the critic who wrote it.

Of course I can, that was me, I wrote it, no, I didn't, my teenage self did, he did. Something scribbled for some essay to annoy a teacher (I am a genius).

"This is patently not Shakespeare's meaning, have you even read my notes? (Silence.) Please, Jesus, listen to me, we've been going over this every Wednesday. I see you sitting there every class, don't think I don't, staring out the window like a gombeen. Why are you not taking this seriously? (Silence.) Once you leave here life won't be so easy, what you do now is preparation for the rest of your life, you do understand that do you not?"

"I understand nothing."

". . . You . . . AMADAN!"

Suppose I do not want to think about ghosts for a change. Have you thought about that, sir? Goodbye. The sound of silence—Simon and Garfunkel never lived in a dead valley like this. How does the night bring more silence? simple and thick, like it could burst with sound if pierced—it is altogether a different quality of silence to that found in the day.

12.

I stuck a sausage in the open jaw of my skull, like it was Groucho Marx or someone chewing on a cigar. I quickly removed it in case the other was watching. I forget myself. From the other's perspective, what I had done could be seen as disrespectful, and they might attack, overnight, but in the daylight I feel good.

13.

The other is deaf, and possibly female. That is what I have deduced. Those hands, "not even the wind has such small hands," yes, and surely that was polish on those shining fingernails. But what is the meaning of the skull? I leave it outside the tent each night, on the path where I first found it: a demonstration of ownership: not mine, it says, I don't know what's happening, it says. Please, it says, please, it kneels, its poor head bowed.

Yorick! Aha, I couldn't resist, alas. The sun is not so hot today. I will investigate the edges on the north side. Crawling? maybe. The palms are so receptive to experience, so many senses to discover. What better way to find those hands than with mine own hands.

Stupid nettles. I repeat, I understand nothing. Nothing!

14.

This night I am in love. It was my third relationship. It almost brought us to the altar to stand beside each other, and vow to live and love together forever. A priest, and flower shop, had been consulted, churches visited. There were other relationships, though not very many; it is the third that binds my love.

The remembrance of what must be reality is devastating. It rips through me. The fire of London has nothing on the slow destruction found in any one life. I will leave this memory here in the valley, let it grow among its family. But this is only a shard of the pain. The tip of the spear, I am a dying man breaking off the tip that points out through his chest, the rest sunk inside him.

15.

. . . I watched the shadows fingercreeping across the stones, and rather than scurrying back to my tent as I usually do, I teased them, stood in wait, and at the last second, stepped back. We played our game across the width of the valley. They caught me in the end, my back up against the far steep slope, and covered me, starting with my feet until I was dressed in darkness and night. That's usually when the other visits and we talk, me with my voice, they with hands and sinewy fingers. The skull sits beside us and talks, too, shadows working on those ivory jaws. I ask them what they know of grief, what they know of me. The skull is a particularly good listener. There was once so much inside it. And now all those memories and pieces of being are gone. They must be the valley. Just like me now and if I am never rescued. Oh, what if I annoyed my driver and he refuses to collect me! Such a stubborn mule of a man, I will break his neck some day, I swear.

16.

It would be so easy to have lost this skull, to say it was once mine in that most personal of ways: the house of my cognition, my fireproof archive, my poor head. Suppose I had been murdered once. Here in the hard valley, for reasons I have yet to know. I could discover these reasons, the motive, and continue with my life, away from here. Surely that is grief enough for one man.

17.

I saw the other killed. Down they went and a new other ran the length of the valley and away. They might have been a grey-hound, those long strides, or the evening shadow running a new direction leaving me in the light. There was no way to follow even if that was something I might have done. Just as I could not outrun the turning of this earth, the sun's golden reach. No. There is nothing for me to discover here. I am as empty as this valley, and the sky is no better. Foolish to the grave. A great big foolish flourish.

18.

The skull listened again last night, and the other—that lithe killer. This one had no visible hands. We have decided we will build a structure in memory to the downed other. I am unsure of this new other's gender. No hands. No face. Everything else. (I drift back to myself when I am away from them.)

(We moaned and mourned, and the morning came and it felt good to see the light it brought, so original and clean.) Gray clouds provide me with our aim this morning: a set of stone stairs climbing away from this valley. It will be a place for others to live inside and live in memory of the others who have gone inside the hard ground.

We cannot lift the boulder beside which I keep my water so

I work in circles, so I work from small to big. I wear my jacket despite the heat, and take up the smallest pebbles first. No bigger than fingernails. Place one in my pocket and move on, disregarding those larger ones until later. The longer it takes, the longer—

I sometimes wake and wonder this valley and myself and the skull. I could be either.

19.

A tourist visiting the grief of his past. He strolls through those squares that once were so traumatic, and as tourists do, stands in silence, waiting for the awe, aching to feel just like they once did, unable to escape the things of their present life. I have been in many galleries and watched patrons search for feeling. Whatever it is that provokes that recognition is rare. I wonder if the artists ever felt anything, or was it valleys like this that gave them their scenes. Was it in valleys like this where anguish roared like rivers? Must have been. The past, of course, was once the present, and anguish, of course, roars through the present, rolling over and over like some horrible tidal wave leaving desolation in its wake, always in the present, always destroying.

20.

How do people drive past those tiny dead bodies. How can anyone live like this? I can't go back to that! I can't live here! It's wrong . . . everywhere. I used to camp with friends when I was very little. Lying here, I could be then, yes, for a little while now I will be then, and, and the valley, the life, my driver, my life, they will be, but now, I am then, safe and past, almost sleeping, dark with grief.

Rigor Terra

THE CONCEPT OF INCARCERATION IS widely acknowledged to have developed around the time language was first taken from our tongues and carved in stone. The oldest written language dates from 900 BCE, and measures 36 x 21 x 13 cm. This stone tablet, discovered by road builders in 1994 in what was once the heartland of the Olmec culture in Mexico, depicts sixty-two signs. Mary Pohl, an expert on this ancient culture notes, "We see that the writing is very closely connected with ritual . . . occurring in the context of the development of a centralised power and stratified society." Written language enabled societies to strengthen their boundaries, enabled the recording of penal codes, enabled the construction of the first penal institutions, and thus built, gave man the power to imprison his fellow man without fear of retribution, something he had been dying to do since his feet first touched the sand, since he first entered through the earth's creaking gates. Man has only ever emulated that which surrounds him, that which I will escape by this day's end.

The bicycle path blurs gray against the steady blackness of my front tyre; looking down like this is dizzying. I look up to find terra stiff as death all round. These roads, these trees, this path on which I cycle will soon be sea. This metal frame and its slick accoutrements, will, by a process of deduction, be a yacht, a canoe, a surfboard and sail. And there will be no prescribed roads or paths from which you can never stray too far from, just this greater Salt Sea water coolly wrapping this earth, surrounding what are really many islands. Out there, across the whale's acre, this voyage will freely venture.

Cycling: the very nature of the exercise is so numbingly circular. I strive to be free in my mind while my body toils, still miles from that salt air. I think of the reproduction of Hawaiian surfers, produced by Émile Bayard, which hangs in my hallway, just above where I once stored my bicycle. On the right, a dark-skinned man, his hands raised above his head as if in fear or jubilation, wearing a white swimsuit, rides a curling wave which when it breaks, as it is in the process of doing, will surely follow that of its siblings, which crash against heavy jutting cliffs in the centre of the image. In the bottom right corner, two men manoeuvre a board up a section of rock that slides into the angry water. One supports the board on his shoulder while the other appears to be about to lower himself on to it. Beside them, and higher up, another is already sitting on his board, sliding down the smooth rock, as nervous as any tourist looking down on the vista of a water park from the top of a tall slide. His companion cheers him on. The surfers are joyous despite the dangers that lie waiting behind so many possible and, at the time, seemingly slight misjudgements. They are alive, at least. Not pummelled by an invisible force, not exhausted by dreary roads and buildings and public parks that are all the same in the least pleasurable way, not cycling through an Irishman's version of purgatory.

After turning right at a busy junction, pedalling hard so as not to be overtaken, and possibly crushed, by an unseeing driver, I feel slightly safer and my thoughts drift to said Irishman's description of the inherent pathology of certain bicycles: "The behaviour of a bicycle that has a high content of humanity, he said, is very cunning and entirely remarkable. You never see them moving by themselves but you meet them in the least accountable places unexpectedly. Did you never see a bicycle leaning against the dresser of a warm kitchen when it is pouring outside?" I did! And did you know about the very first bicycle? I do. Baron von Drais created it. His *Laufmaschine* has unceasingly built my cell walls since 1817. The wooden frame of the

Laufmaschine, or *draisienne*, is no more than the large body of a rifle, sharpening to a point at which it will shear the wind with bullets. Affixed beneath this point is the wheel, and accordingly another wheel is set behind the seating area, which, at the time of creation, had yet to become a saddle. The ghost of that first machine resides inside the hollow aluminium frame beneath me. I will twist these metal bars until they can support a sail, something that will welcome the wind, and bellow, and snap pleasingly into shape when engulfed by that rude, elemental force. The wind bloweth where it listeth, but there are no mountains for breezes to slide down together and skip across the dirty city to gather at your face, and chest, so impertinently in the sea. Of course one of the most integral components of the bicycle is the saddle; when we are tired we can sit. And yet the presence of this seat cannot stop us from falling once we resolve to stop pressing forward.

And what about the pedals?

They are manacles about my feet.

Successful escapees must study their environment in order to discover the best escape routes. I have studied well, and in doing so, discovered the true extent of our imprisonment by prisons, bicycles, the land I cycle upon, and every solid thing in between. I have relied heavily on the writings of Anderson Hassett, three-time Tour de France winner (1983, 1984, 1988), now leader of the freedom movement. He was one of the first to describe the psychic prisons which everyday objects build around their owners after many repetitions of usage:

> The user becomes trapped by the functional limitations of their tool and so the tool becomes the jailer. A prime example of this type of imprisonment can be witnessed in the cyclist. To the uninitiated the bicycle promises vast horizons of freedom. You can cycle as far as your legs will carry you, and farther still after a rest and healthy snack. Yet, you cannot propel yourself with your arms, or decide you would like to cycle with your feet up on the crossbar.

To deviate from what is the prescribed function is to be
unable to cycle; this in essence is imprisonment, for what is
imprisonment if it is not the freedom to do as you please.

Though he does not go as far as I do (few have), it can be
deduced that anything derived from the ground will contain
within its being those ingredients necessary for imprisonment.
Wherever there is earth a prison can, and will, be made; it is the
stuff of confinement. And yes, the written word is among the
most impenetrable of prisons, whether on paper, stone, computer screen, or gable wall. And yes, these words will be left
behind me on the dull shore just as the stench of a confined
man, his sweat-stained bedclothes, his ragged dreams are left
behind in his suddenly empty jail cell.

While the terra is a prison, there are parts of this world which
remain free. The air allows its molecules to move as they please,
but we cannot live among the clouds. The freest habitable environment on this earth, therefore, is the sea.

I have read so much about the sea, the place of our first birth,
our watery Eden. We still carry it with us. Depending on the person, it is said we are mostly composed of water—from slightly
more than half to more than three-quarters—yet when you
open us up it is disguised, dyed red, hidden amongst the messy
flesh and innards. We thought we left it one day, back when we
couldn't think or talk or be, but it came along with us, the parent of the prodigal children, who instead of waving us off, snuck
along in our suitcase, inside us, and we know it, or at least the
older of us do, when they speak of advice given to them by their
waters. I sometimes feel like I am the only one who recognises
the need, the desire, to go back. I feel an affinity with the earliest
wave riders; they understood better than we do. In the fifteenth
century, the Sandwich Islanders practiced the art and religion
of *he'e nalu*—wave sliding. *He'e* translates as "the change from
a solid form to a liquid form," thus encapsulating our essential
need for freedom. *Nalu* is more complicated. The first letter, *N*,
recalls the initial difficulty in mounting the wave: the tip of the
tongue is pressed behind the top front teeth, the centre of the

tongue rises, emulating the swelling of the wave; the vocal cords vibrate—the sea's rumbling kinetic energy—and the tongue is released: the wave has been mounted. The pronunciation of *alu* elegantly replicates the final release of the wave as the tongue is held momentarily in the centre of the mouth, untouched by the surrounds, before sliding against the gum behind the top teeth then racing through the now pursed lips, riding the air until the breath is gone and the surfer is left empty on the shore with the damp sand and shiny pebbles. I once sat among the dunes, listening to the dry grass rustle in the singing wind, and rumbling low beneath it, the bass of the sea's dark moan. This time I will go farther, I will breach the walls of this prison, ride past those great breaking waves, let the tide carry me free, free of reason, free of humanity.

Look, see those trees I now cycle past; forget the immediate perceptions: autumn leaves spread across the grass in front of each trunk imitating the sunlight that once nurtured them, the sunlight that draws for each tree a shadow each evening, forget that. Nothing is imitating anything. The best thing to do right now is exchange those leaves and trees for the cries of waves, and white gulls bobbing, or buoys, so far out there is no need for categories or thought. A squirrel throws its slack body from the branches above me in a leafy explosion. Momentarily distracted, my hands allow the front wheel to drift from its steady course. I turn back to the road just in time to avoid the back of a van parked in my lane: an inanimate prison warden placed in my way.

Now see the riverrunning through the city to the sea, just ahead of me. I cannot compete with its easy flow: the wind fights my every pedal. I remember watching a video of Dublin, circa 1970, on the internet. The city looks unusual at first and then you realise why, it is that bicycles outnumber cars. The early-, middle-, and latter-aged of the population can be seen in various uniforms atop their bicycles, enchained between their two wheels without knowing it. The wind, though invisible, reveals itself by its cruel humour: a lifted hat landing before a bus, the flippant hem of an otherwise modest dress, a drooping coat-tail about to catch in that office worker's back spokes. Having no mass it defeats us before we can put on our armour, before we have slid inside our underamour. Those same bicycles now rot in forgotten sheds, beneath towering mounds of household waste. They have been transformed. They are flaking rust, torn leather, burnt rubber.

While I look forward to living among the waves, I am also worried. I was never baptised. My parents have always failed to explain their reasoning, and I fear this, for water is most abundant, and I fear what will happen on my arrival at the shore. Countless surfers have been spat out. The ones it has taken were rarely ready to go. "You see, that's what the sea does, and you want to trust your life to the sea?" I am borne by my inner currents, ceaselessly borne back. Now look at me. I have barely fashioned the vessel that will carry me away, these wheels are still wheels, these handle bars will not propel me through waves and storms that take place far from land. I am not yet ready for that rough mosaic of seagull cries and salt. Oh the sea! The sea is everything. Is that not where Edmond Dantès escaped to, where Lord Jim always escaped to, where I must escape to, away from the terror that is land, that is our prison? I spy seagulls now; it is near, I can almost smell it.

As I pedal past sad flats with their multi-coloured playgrounds, I replay voices whose messages were of great comfort to me. I hear the heavily accented English of a Frenchman, a voice that could only mature in 1956: "This building is the military prison at Montluc, in Lyon. In 1943, in this world of cement and iron, under the watch of the Nazis, a man escaped. One. Lieutenant André Devigny." I hear the upper-class English accent that is shorthand for ancient epic Greece and Rome: "Behold! human beings living in a underground den, which has a mouth open towards the light and reaching all along the den; here they have been from their childhood, and have their legs and necks chained so that they cannot move, and can only see before them, being prevented by the chains from turning round their heads." (Later, we could not bear to imagine Plato's prisoners being chained in a den, a place of our own making, and so the den became a cave, a natural feat which happened to enchain us: the terra of an alien place condemning us trespassers.) Now the voice is that of Dostoevsky's unnamed character: "The favourite occupation of one of the convicts, during the moments of liberty left to him from his hard labour, was to count the palisades. There were fifteen hundred of them. He had counted them all, and knew them nearly by heart. Every one of them represented to him a day of confinement; but, counting them daily in this manner, he knew exactly the number of days that he had still to pass in the prison." And finally, my ancestor in spirit, Captain Nemo, Captain Nobody: "I am not what you call a civilized man! I have done with society entirely, for reasons which I alone have the right of appreciating. I do not therefore obey its laws, and I desire you never to allude to them before me again!"

Windsurfing is a relatively recent offshoot of surfing. It is this that I will do, at first; in the beginning. I will paddle, sail, and lie on my board unconstrained until I can swim without end. At one stage, windsurf boards were the fastest wind-powered vessels found on the surface of the glittering sea. At speed, the board skips between each small wave so that there is a constant slapping that becomes a machine-gun rattle at higher speeds. I will lean so far back, pulling the sail between the winds unleashed from the stables of Aeolus and the board, leaning so close together we become a spear thrown by Aeolus along the water's surface, skittering between the immobile continents, those leering fortresses. Apart from the meeting of the board and sea, there is silence at such high speed when facing forward, but if you turn your head to either side, the wind will pierce your ears. Out there, you have a choice that is not available on land: you can join in the wind's endless odyssey, or suffer.

These thin bicycle tyres cut up will make a safe harness so I can affix myself to the sail and have my arms free. For now, they trammel wet leaves as I cycle to my voyage. Here I must concentrate as I pass through this narrow gate with its preceding, and now succeeding, fence posts whumping past—incidentally, I know their number by heart. Yes, I have a harness, and frame for my sail, and clothes to make the sail itself. What I need is a board. I will take one of these trees, a broad and dumb trunk to carve on my way. Now look at me. I am ready for my freedom.

It waits at the top of the city. The wind slows my wheels as if it were composed of countless grudges. The traffic screeches and rumbles in my ears. Buses drive too close, and I feel I could too easily swerve into their hot sides, or the kerb, which might throw me to the path's relative safety, or throw me against those hot sides. The traffic lights flash red and I am grateful to stop, to rest, for now. There is still a considerable distance between myself and my destination. A distance made greater by many subtle hills, which in my exhausted state might as well be waves off storm-carved Sligo, waves bearing me backward, like a piece of driftwood, like some straggling piece of seaweed, bearing me backward down their magnificent, sloping shoulders, bearing me downward as the tide recedes into its many silent caves far beneath the surface of the saltwater sea.

An Urgent Letter to the Reader Regarding a Moment from the Life of Fyodor Dostoevsky

WHEN I THINK OF YOU, the reader, as you read this—I rarely do think of you, I admit, but when I do—and think of myself, when I will have written this, when my thoughts will have come together again, freed from the demand of the other, free to continue, free to try to avoid continuing gathering all of myself into a hardened knot, thinking that which I do not want to think about—hopefully I'll be able to return to this (these words), and picture you reading me, because if I write this in my own way, these words will create, as if from putty, the physiognomy of my mind, or so Schopenhauer says, and, through reading, your thoughts might rest inside mine for a moment while our bodies remain distant (this will happen as often as someone reads these words: I am not faithful and I am serious)—but now I hope to think of other things (our tentative relationship has grown too close to those thoughts I want to avoid, and I type that word with care, I do, because the removal of just one letter leaves me open to that . . . which I will not allow myself to think about) I must find some distraction: Why is it considered crass to address you, the reader? am I to pretend I am not aware of another reading this, despite every piece of submitted writing being a letter, first to an editor, and then, hopefully, to another? is it that the "I" when writing is not the "I" when speaking (and is this why so many persist in writing "i," that which embodies the ultimate false modesty, that lethargic evasion of the question of "I"), is it that by addressing the reader the author contradicts the act of writing? like how dare he write so directly on behalf of the writing? like does he not realise that he is not the writing, that the writing is the obliteration of his ability to say I? like the writing is a shadow of his coming death no, no—this brings me back to those previous thoughts; I look away from the screen, stop typing, see the calendar on my desk, it reads December 22, and this being a literary calendar (given to me as a gift last year . . . I mean to say, a gift that is about to lose its utility, forcing me to choose whether to replace it, throw it away, or store it in a drawer to forget) I read three sentences which tell me that in 1849, on this day, Fyodor Dostoevsky stood on a damp flagstone, or his feet straddled two of them, in Moscow, before a line of five, perhaps four, who knows how many—six men all armed and ready to shoot him—that young man who at that time had barely written a novel, who had published a couple of short stories, who had not yet lost his hair—and this feels much better (I would thank you, my reader, even though it is not your doing, but it is, too, in a way, I feel thankful, I will say my thanks undirected so as to spare your embarrassment, let my thanks drift past you; watch it go and do not try to keep it, let it live alone): each time I recall Fyodor Dostoevsky I am again astonished at the overwhelming success of his work, as everything I have read about him tells me he suffered enough for four, if not six, men, a village of men, a continentful, no, not that much, a village then, so it is good to know he made the world hurt in some way: I mean, he is known by every literate person over the age of fifteen, and has been for the past ninety, if not more, years; he holds the honour of having been amongst those, otherwise celebrated, authors dismissed by Vladimir Nabokov (who writes of one of Dostoevsky's novels: it is "a rather mediocre one—with flashes of excellent humour, but, alas, with wastelands of literary platitudes in between"); and the enduring popularity of his novella *Notes from Underground* among adolescents who wear black and hate their parents for not letting them paint their bedroom walls and ceiling black is especially wondrous: all this comes to mind, and, of course is

followed, as youth follows youth, by my experience as a young
adolescent learning to despair, reading the whole of *Crime and
Punishment* in a day during a summer heat wave when the water
was stopped and I, sweating, eating melting ice cream, burned
in sympathy with Raskolnikov—this occurred when this writer
was not yet a writer but a happy reader—but now that I think
of Fyodor, and of his precariment on this day so many years ago,
I imagine that this sensitive, idealistic Russian, as he stands
before the firing squad, has already involuntarily reviewed his
life thus far (this has never happened to me, but I have never
been moments before my death—I have often wondered if this
condensed history is only reviewable when the certainty of death
is complete, or does it begin and is it just as suddenly cut off
when death is averted? say when a car breaks just that bit too
late, just enough to bruise your shin), and having used up a
second or two in this life-review, there must be a number of
seconds remaining before the triggers are pulled and five, or
perhaps six, a rain of bullets travel across the courtyard in light
rain (yes), between falling snow (who knows, they might indeed
become replicant suns beneath a higher one—whatever the
weather they will definitely), pierce Doestoevsky's clothes, and
very soon afterward, his skin; oh no; God no: I am suddenly
aware of the worst possibility—my world has just been split
open, my heart, no, my world, no, I have just seen the split, no,
I have just remembered our stepping, yes oh no, yes, all of us,
what we call humanity, stepping off the edge of the chasm and
have remembered we are not now standing but perpetually falling, that those are the walls of the earth surrounding us as we
fall, as we fall and our feet will be crushed, obliterated when we
land but we won't even feel this, because we will all have disappeared, obliterated, all of us, and this solves some of my problems, that is true, it does, but it creates so many more that I
might as well be an ant beneath a child's fat, descending foot,
an ant squished and seen falling from the heel in that chubby
foot's ascent, and you are no better, reader; you see, having
recently read some of the more avant-garde articles from the
scientific literature, and keeping in mind Fyodor's immeasurable

success since that day, and underlining it all: the date in which I write these words, I have just now arrived at a conclusion that might scare you, it might shock you, but I don't care, it doesn't matter how you feel, and you will soon see why, you would die for the problem of a rude author in a minute, that's how bad this is, you would die to have the problems of the world, to have anything, just to be able to experience, to live, I suppose, when you hear what I have to say; in a moment everything has been lost, and all thanks to an arid desert of an insight, a world of forever sweeping sands of an insight, you will see, you will see why there is no reason why either of us should care about any-thing, because having considered this over the time it has taken to write what you have read (and it has taken much more time to write than it must to read, unless you read a word a day, and I doubt that), I believe it is probable, and especially so when it is remembered that the quality of the creative mind, the mind of a writer—surely Fyodor Dostoevsky possesses one—is said to be infinite, and, having read about similar occurrences, and con-sidering that this seemingly short span of time might appear to last an eternity during the last moments of one's life, any indi-vidual's mind will inevitably turn, at this fatal moment, to what is about to be stolen from him: I am sure Dostoevsky is now thinking about his future; and this, if you have not yet aban-doned me (and I don't care if you have), this is where I home in on my conclusion, because, all this time, I have been aiming at this point, even if the evidence reads otherwise, and I admit it does when I read back over what has been written, and it was, actually, I was going to write—no—yes, yes, I am sorry about that (in fact I am not, you are nothing); but bearing in mind the infinite quality of the creative mind (because I do want you to understand, if only to free you, too, so I will not be alone in my understanding), it is my supposition that I, the writer, and you, the reader, and this, our world, and everything we know, feel, and have done, including the almost unimaginable literary suc-cess of a young man from Moscow, including the two World Wars, and all those other ones in between and still ongoing, the genocides, the killings, the beatings, the unethical practices of

almost everyone, and including, of course, the creature that is
Vladimir Nabokov (not that I consider Nabokov to be a part of
the previous category of horrors, it is just that he is Nabokov,
you understand), all of it is born of Dostoevsky's fevered mind;
if evidence were required one need only picture this our cruel
and stupid future to realise it could only have been invented by
a depressed utopist facing his death—if you are not yet per-
suaded, not fully, then it must be remembered that most characters do not know they live in novels; we are not even in a novel,
we are the result of a few seconds' thought from a man facing a
firing squad, we cannot blame him for getting so many details
wrong in his imagining of us, and in a time so far in the future!
and you must not be too harsh in your judgement of my imagining his precarious position, he is, essentially, our God (the
unknown and the invisible, the visible and the known, and every
other thing), I believe that any minute now, any second now
because it is quite difficult to guess just when those bullets will
sink inside him and who knows how long the imagination can
continue after such an event, but any moment now, or soon, in
the future, perhaps (I say perhaps a lot, don't I? I swear I barely
say it when I speak, then I say maybe, maybe too much, but
when I write I almost always prefer perhaps, strange, isn't it, that
Dostoevsky thought all the way down to this silly detail, don't
you think?), it might even be a hundred years from now (sorry
I am very nervous)—perhaps each millisecond of a man's last
moments contain a hundred years, and so we might live even
longer than I previously supposed—but one day for us, albeit
on December 22, 1849, for him, Fyodor Dostoevsky will fall to
the ground and die (and he will never have written *The Brothers
Karamazov*, *The House of the Dead*, and so on, and the world will
have been spared Woody Allen's nasal invocations of those tortured syllables that make up this Muscovite's name), and life in
mid-eighteenth-century Russia will happily carry on, and that
will be the end of us and everything we hate and care for; it will
be as if we had never existed, because we didn't, we don't.

Detachment

I also am other than what I imagine myself to be.
                                                    —Simone Weil

1.

BY THE LEFT WALL A red camping stove balances on what might be a small fridge; from this wall a short line of clothes strings above a bed on which the man sits with his hands on his knees. His head is bowed, as if in prayer, the chin resting on the chest. Photos, or postcards, are pinned to the wall behind him; from this distance they are blotches of colour: beige, green, blue on the bare wall. He wears a T-shirt that might once have been white. If he were to stand he may hit his head on the bulb, or catch a damp black sock with his forehead.

Outside, on the path, the voyeur was woken from this scene by the sudden presence of another, a man who grabbed his arm. This was always embarrassing. Returning to himself he would strain his thoughts for an activity: solving a problem, examining something; to do nothing felt wrong, childish, somehow. To do nothing is to hint at a secrecy. And it is worse when one is standing: to stand and do nothing is very sinister (unless one queues, that is). He experienced this initial embarrassment when he felt that hand on his arm, but the nature of the hold, the strength that clamped, made him fearful. It startled him. Give me your wallet, perv, the man said (almost casually). He did as asked, his fingers thick and fumbling. The man shoved an elbow in his stomach. He stumbled, tripped on the curb, and fell backward, his body collapsing against the concrete.

That ignorant thug should not have called him that, that thug obviously did not have the refinement necessary to understand the pleasure of watching, that . . . thug! What he did was voyeuristic, yes, but that word does not deserve the connotations that have sunk it to the depth of the insult. Supposedly, to be a voyeur is to be a pervert, but he was not that: it was not genitals or infidelities that excited him—primarily, it should be said, because of course they did, too—it was the chance to see someone as they are, that was all.

He would not have remembered the aftermath of his being robbed—the strange shape of his body as he fell—if this had not been shown to him by the police in a large and poorly lit room in a nearby station. The room had smelt of sweat and lemons. He didn't remember how he got there. They said he was unconscious when they arrived at the scene, but they did not mention his being brought to a hospital, nor having seen a doctor. They were suspicious, so much so that he felt his own suspicions were not allowed to surface; there was not enough room for his trite fears and imaginings among these tired men in their uniforms inside their place of work. They were busy, and just trying to do their job, they said when he asked about his injury. They kept asking—varying their words as if the right combination might unlock his truth—why he had stood outside that house. At first he had said he was checking his phone for the time. They proved this wrong by showing him CCTV footage on a large screen. Standing there on the empty path, he seemed to shed his self of life until he was a lengthening shadow among many others on that quiet road. The time rolled on to three minutes as he stared through the window on the screen and he could feel the heat gathering in his cheeks as the police watched him watch his self; luckily the thug darted into the frame from the right and, within less than half a minute, having grabbed him, accepted his wallet, shoved him, crouched beside him, dipped inside his trouser pockets, disappeared out of the frame on the left—drawing his and their attention into the screen's dark side.

He ignored the fact of his stillness, his staring, and asked if the police knew where this thug had gone. He called the man that, and they did not correct him, so he continued to use this word. He enjoyed the abrupt feel of it, how it felt almost like spitting. The officer opened a new window on the screen and together they watched the thug pause two streets away to inspect the wallet and a phone that he recognised as missing from his pocket. The thug walked free of the frame. The footage stuttered, and there was a new street: the thug emerged from the darkness at the top of the screen, sauntering behind, then past, a boy and girl who held hands and walked very slowly. He continued out of frame. Had he been about to rob them, too? Or did their presence, the presence of their affection, inspire feelings other than hatred, greed, or whatever it was that motivated the thug to rob him? He noticed the thug's shabby jacket, the way he limped with his left leg. He remembered that face, blunt and hardened. A face worn down to its base features. Like a cliff, he thought, and him, the broken ship beneath it. Another street, with more shops, busier; it took a while to spot the thug in the crowd. A succession of cameras captured and released him as he walked through the city until no camera could find him. The police suspected he had disappeared down an alley. They said it led inside a complex of flats, with at least five other exits. They hadn't managed to pick the man up on any camera. There are cameras everywhere in the city, they said, when he asked how they could follow the thug so easily. On his walk home he saw these cameras, and they saw him, but who it was at the end of that process, they could not be seen, they who sat behind the lens watching the windows to the city on their screens.

2.

There was a necessary risk in his voyeurism: he did not hide. He stood in the dark as the other was in the light; sharing in their vulnerability, open to their seeing him. If he had purposefully made himself indistinguishable from the scene outside lighted windows and open doorways, camouflaged himself in some way, temporarily or more permanently, it would not have been fair on the person he watched. There was a contract between them, one he had effectively signed and had always held out to the other so that they would see it if they were to look up from themselves. To hide would have been akin to bustling them along the contract like a pushy salesman: no need to read all this legalese, leave that to the lawyers, eh? Just sign here, and here, and just there, and you'll be driving away in your new car in no time! The presence of those cameras on every street in the city, in every public building—the thought made him dizzy, fragile with anxiety (and those jitters, that unsteadiness of body and purpose became increasingly frequent visitors). There was no fairness in that indiscriminate recording.

A front door opens, waking a house from a row of sleeping buildings. A man (white shirt, black tie untied), exits, carrying something large and dark in his arms; he walks to the side of the house, out of view. The hall is framed by the open doorway. Green walls. A short brown lamp on a side table. Dark wood stairs of which can be seen the last few steps. A foot appears, then another, and again, and again, until there is a woman wearing a pale robe—loosely tied. Pulling a protective arm around her waist, she sits on the fourth step. She rests a phone on her knees, which are pressed together. She looks at the screen, then out toward the night. She slams the phone against the wall beside her. Again, and again, and the expression on her face is difficult to see from this distance, but the thuds—they thud. The man reappears, jogging, his arms now empty. He stares across the street, glances at the neighbouring houses, and returns inside. The door closes.

He watched only to see the person as they really are, to see them unfolded, human, alone: a perspective neither their friends nor their family, not even the seemingly intimate reflection of the mirror, would ever witness. Something not meant to be seen, but not hidden. Mundane activities became streets in a labyrinthine city he had only just entered: this person may be sitting on an armchair reading their phone or watching television, but not knowing this person, anything might happen. They might swerve at any moment. But those cameras, they did not care about who they watched, they cared only for behaviours, actions, evidence; that there was a person behind this externality was not important. They demolished labyrinths, killed mystery. They reduced him. These were not the benevolent eyes of statues, or voyeurs, but eyes that report things deemed suspicious, nosy eyes that seek difference.

He had read an essay about the use of quarantine when plague was suspected of having entered a town, of having parked its mouldering black carriage in someone's home. A militia, made up of "good officers and men of substance," are positioned at the town's gates, by the town hall, and at the end of every street in every quarter, so as to observe the residents who cannot leave the town. If the residents try to leave they will be killed. At the initial suspicions of a plague having entered this small section of society, a list of residents is compiled, with their sex, age, weight, illnesses, and anything "of note" recorded.

On certain days, they cannot even leave their homes, if they do they will be killed. Inspections are made: each resident having been previously assigned a window in their home. At a certain time each day a representative of this newly formed law stops before each home and calls out the names of the inhabitants. At each call, the inhabitant must appear in their prescribed window to reveal their continuing health: he found this both comical and depressing, the reduction of the human to a jack-in-the-box: Pop! goes the weasel. This search for the plague is not too different from the history of the jack-in-the-box, which is said to have begun when a prelate cast the devil inside a boot to protect his village (in England, naturally). These men of substance were looking for the devil in those windows, regardless of whether it lived inside a neighbour or friend. And this particular devil must be cast out because the plague, of course, cannot be banished inside a boot.

If the resident who stands in their prescribed window does not answer the representative's questions truthfully, they will be killed. If they do not appear at the window when called, the men will enter the house and remove that person and every other person from the house. What is done with these, the most unfortunate of the unfortunate, he wasn't sure. But now, a sentence is remembered as if it were wholly new. It will now become new as it appears in the context of these memories: "Each individual is continually assessed in order to determine whether he conforms to the rule, to the defined norm of health."

There was no difference between this militia made of men of substance and those cameras. In fact, the author made a similar point about surveillance, though that author could not have foreseen cities overgrown with cameras, cameras that sprout like weeds from the sides of buildings, from ceilings, strangling their carefully composed features. A few years before his mugging, he saw a young girl walk through the exit of a shop. Seconds later, two burly men raced after the girl, one jumping in front of her, the other to the side, ready to apprehend. He couldn't hear what was said, but they jostled her back inside the shop and through a door he had never noticed. He had felt ill at the speed of the events and, at the same time, slightly superior to her. The officiousness and righteousness of the men's movements led him—while they led the girl—to take her guilt as a certainty. At the time he forgot the scene immediately, though it often came to him when he was about to exit a shop: a brief fear that seconds later he would be apprehended and taken back inside despite his being sure of his innocence. This was perhaps the first of those moments he can remember when he was unsure who he was, unsure about what exactly he knew about himself. His earliest memory of self-questioning.

Those bouncers probably replayed footage, of what looked like the girl stealing some item, in that hidden room. And by making her—the girl, the quivering innocent who has stolen—watch this, she is forced to pass judgement on herself. That girl there, on the screen there, she is guilty of having stolen: she is a criminal, lock her up, the girl finds herself saying, unable to say anything other, having witnessed this scene so often in films, and reality television, that she is almost conditioned to apportion blame. The video ends, and she finds herself an innocent again, wakened from the dream of the television, and yet the police are being called now because the bouncers have changed the rules again: she is no longer playing judge, but criminal—the individual must play all of these roles. They must be cleaved in pieces in atonement for the crime of having lived. The word *individual* must be smashed so that the person is finally—divisible—no longer a person. Irretrievable.

How many nature documentaries could be made with the patched-together footage of foxes scraping across city roads at night, crows crowding the tiles of an abandoned house, so that against the evening sky it seemed medieval, seagulls' desperate cries at being so far from the sea they can no longer smell it? How many crime shows are made from the recordings of what were once innocent people?

Through a window a girl slowly dances, and though the window is partially open, no music can be heard. Her eyes are closed, as if she were sleeping. She wears dark jeans, a loose-fitting gray T-shirt, a collection of bangles on her right arm. There are open books, and the pad of a laptop, just visible, on a white desk by the wall on the right. The back wall, that is, the one directly facing the window, is occupied by shelves, filled with books organised by colour (yellow, black, red, blue) and three figurines of swans in three stages from water to flight, placed in a row on the top shelf. The left side of the room cannot be seen, and now she has stopped dancing and is gazing in that direction.

Often, he saw himself cold and pale and placed alongside the object of his gaze, as if he and they were together behind that warm window. It is unfortunate that he lived for these moments when he could lose himself, when he was so close to not existing, when he may as well not have existed for this person who was living, and dreaming, suffering. People are raw then, and that, he thought, was why their shock was so visceral when they spotted him. The frantic movement, the rush for the curtains, the stopped scream; the scream. Breaking glass. As if he had violated them just by his seeing who they are when alone. Is life really so violent that people react like this? Or was it that they, in their silence—when they had reduced themselves "to the point they occupy in time and space," which, as Simone Weil writes, is to reduce one's self to nothing, was it that they, in this moment, had unknowingly accepted death, and he, by his watching, woke them from this, unleashed the world and its fullness back inside them where it could never fit—life never really fits inside the body, not comfortably, how could it? Or was it that in seeing them he saw their secrets, which rise up to the skin when people are fully alone; perhaps it is this that they were afraid of, that he had seen what they really feel, what they think when not even they are present enough to curtail their hidden truths. When they saw him, that still figure, their secrets burrowed back down inside the interior, afraid to emerge again until the curtains were closed, the blinds shut, the light turned off. Perhaps this is why dreams are so full of secrecy. Memories, too.

3.

In the museum he watched the statues and they did not care. He stood very close and observed the fine veins of their hands, the blank gaze of their eyes—pinholes for pupils. He walked around them and they did not move. They dismissed his gaze because past their surface is solidity and rock as hard as when the sculptor first bought a slab that had been taken from deep inside the earth. The eyes of a marble statue gaze out from the darkness of the earth. Their secrets cannot burrow past their surface. Their presence is their secret. Whose bodies were used to model these heroes and gods? Labourers, lovers, models, fellow sculptors—did they, for the time they accepted stillness into their bodies, cease to exist, or did they ruminate on the things of their lives? Their bodies are seen just as they were by the sculpturer, however many centuries ago, and through the sculpturer's gaze it is not the model that is seen but the projection of the artist's vision that rests over that mortal frame.

Almost daily he would watch the woman who also visited the Hall of Sculpture. He watched how she watched the statues, how she touched the ends of the broken arms when she thought nobody was looking, or when she knew it was only he who saw. (They were mostly alone in their devotion.) She was always well dressed, mid-thirties, he thought. Composed. It was usually past midday, lunchtime, when they met like this and they recognised in each other this need to observe. There were no words between them, only this understanding; their flesh among the stone. There was a risk in their not speaking, and an acceptance of this risk. A play between them. Some days she followed him through the room, her heels on the wooden floor clacking, or her soft soles whispering, and she would stand so close he felt the heat of her body against his, a projection, a promise, while he stood before some cold white figure. Relishing the sensation, he would pause before turning. She was always walking away, though her perfume lingered—which sometimes made him sneeze, though he did his best to stifle this impulse. On other days it was he who followed her. Their breathing quickening together. Their heat. Sometimes he wondered if she followed him home, if she continued to watch through his window as he—he, what was it he did when he was alone in those days? (This has already been forgotten it seems, or rather it is not the time to remember just now.) He never allowed himself to follow her home, though he desperately wanted to. Often, he would follow her as far as the cafe by the entrance, watching as she left the museum, debating whether he should just go, find where she worked, and from there . . .

And the statues, he believed they gazed through him searching for the hands that held the chisel, the hands that first stroked their faces. Those eyes gaze back through the centuries to the moment of their creation, everything else—like him and this woman, the corniced walls of the gallery—were shadows falling from their vision. What is it they expect to see? They cannot shift position. They cannot see anyone. How many scenes have passed by the blind eyes of those old statues? How much of man's nature has stumbled before their unseeing gaze? There must be a reason so many look upward.

4.

Three severed heads lying on the floor of his bedroom, for however long he would wake in the early morning believing this is what he would see if he were to turn on the light. The reasoning behind the unnatural distancing of these heads from their bodies rarely stayed the same; each night's dream produced a different story, but all ended in this same way: three severed heads lying on the floor beside his bed. In dreams . . .

IN DREAMS . . .

5.

He could no longer face lighted windows on his long walks through the city nights with the cameras always seeming to be perched a few feet above him wherever he found a promising opening of curtains. There was no hiding one's nature from them, not when one was still living. They had seen him walk to the shop to buy milk each evening, go to the cinema, the museum, had watched as he glanced at shop windows, at the faces of those who passed him, at the bodies of those in front of him. There was so little of him that wasn't recorded. Did it matter that they were not in his home? He lived so little there. The hours spent in his apartment were short gaps in the greater pattern of his archive, easily filled with a little imagination.

And the thought of some city personnel watching him from a desk, flitting from his still form to the countless other scenes sprawling across his or her monitor—like a distant parent. He questioned himself, or he questioned his motives, whether his actions were those of a person he would admit to being while under oath, before a jury of his peers (what peers? his peers are the dead). And even when that false parent was at home, sleeping, those blank eyes continued to watch as those statues do, with the difference that their unseeing gaze was recorded, and could be watched by human eyes, eyes that sought. He was constrained by all of these eyes, pinned down by their ubiquity. If the stars could see they would own the earth. The city is not a place for living but a box in which people barely survive, the walls of the box barely walls, so full are they of these fixed eyes. The city is a place of observation. An experiment in existence.

6.

His landlord—a tall and bald man, about mid-sixties—had a penchant for primary-coloured shirts with white collars (a hint of thick gold chain), and had always had a key to his door. Before the mugging, he had barely seen the landlord, aside from their passing each other in the hallway now and then, though he had avoided this when possible. The landlord liked to talk about himself, and his achievements, which included five heart attacks. It seemed that soon after the mugging the landlord began entering his apartment. He would open the door and walk through the rooms, whistling sometimes—a tune that cannot be remembered. The landlord never seemed surprised by his tenant's presence, or even ashamed at being found snooping. He would complain about this intrusion, and the landlord would say: Just checking—with a little smile dwarfed by his large monolithic face, his indifferent eyes—and leave.

He didn't know how to respond to this, and he couldn't affix another lock on the door without the landlord's permission. He tried asking, but the request was denied, with a note that said that it would be a safety hazard. He wrote further emails which weren't replied to. He wrote letters and no response. Every time he heard steps outside his door he froze, sick with the thought it was him, that he might enter and he would be unable to do anything. He asked the other tenants about the situation, but no one said they had any problems, apart from the cost of the rent, and the smell of rotting food that tended to drift in through opened windows. It was atrocious the way the landlord treated him, but by the landlord's doing so, it seemed the landlord was in the right, yet he knew this was wrong, but the landlord appeared so calm and assured.

He rehearsed conversations between them until he successfully made his points, but in these imaginary conversations, the landlord invariably questioned him about his voyeurism, and he became muddled as he tried to explain the difference between what he did—his hobby, it could be called—and what the landlord was doing to him. If anything, what he did to people he didn't know was worse, the landlord always said in these conversations. It was only at times when he was quiet, barely thinking, close to sleep or daydreaming, that it would come to him why what he did was natural, actually a sign of one's humanity, something to be expected, no matter a person's morality, but these reasonings were mostly cloudy and diffuse, changing shape the minute he tried to store them in readiness for the next invasion.

7.

Too many cameras. At windows, he only glanced and continued walking, shortening his gaze to an inch, lessening what he saw so that he was no better than a camera scanning the window, watching without knowing what he was looking at until he had passed, too late to understand what had been seen. A cafe by his work took prominence. It was safe, watching in the cafe, sitting at an unstable table on the wide pavement. The coffee was always burnt, and the milk too hot: safe. One coffee, thirty minutes: the average time of the other patrons. Sitting any longer would surely catch the attention of the cameras, for the future when he would commit a crime, they would notice he had lingered just that bit too long, and they would put this footage to a new purpose, that of evidence of his already calcifying distinction from the law-abiding people around him: his otherness that was always suspect. But thirty minutes was not enough. In a public space, you need at least that to find the moment when another fully relaxes into their self, and even then, it usually only lasts a few seconds, especially if in a busy area.

When he sat there, aware of the cameras pinning him, and everything he did, inside their insistent gaze—so that he was really unable to see anyone else but the cameras from the sides of his vision, unable to do anything but think, to look back inside himself—he could not help thinking of Louis Malle's *Le Feu Follet*. It follows a writer who has decided he will kill himself, but who tries one last time to find a reason not to when his friend invites him to stay in his apartment in the city. He has not seen the film, and never will, so this synopsis is necessarily second-hand, but there is a scene on YouTube which he once watched enough to have memorised it. Two men have just walked away from a cafe table leaving one man still sitting: the actor who plays the writer. He is left alone and music, Eric Satie's Gnossienne no. 3, begins to play alongside the sounds of the road. The actor is sweating and his movements portray an unease as he watches the people around him. A woman passes, her short blond bob instantly placing the film in the 1960s if this was not already apparent. His gaze follows her path across the expanse of the cafe's large outdoor section. Three ladies pass by, carrying files or folders, probably empty, or borrowed, maybe even scripts for those actors who have to speak: he watches these almost suspiciously. A mother and child and grandmother enter the interior of the cafe. Another woman, she might be a student. A car pulls away from the curb and two incongruous-looking men, twins maybe, both with tanned faces and large teeth filling wide smiles, one wearing sunglasses, the other not, both leering at someone unseen who must still be on the path. Another man, all that can be seen of him is his dark hair, he drives. The twins might even be statues; as the car drives away, the one wearing sunglasses now appears to be gazing at the camera (the other twin's face is obscured now by the back of an extra sitting at a table in front of the actor playing the writer). At the last second, one of the twins waves, breaking the spell of their strangeness. The writer fidgets, looks to his side, leans forward in his chair. A family walk past; now two women, one man, all wearing thick-rimmed glasses. Two women. A girl leans away from her table to watch him, her face on the cusp of a smile, but he does not seem to notice. A couple. A group of young girls. The waiter (white coat, thin black moustache). An elderly man (thick white moustache) looks to either side, sneakily, then grabs the paper-covered straws from their holder on his table and quickly shoves them into his bag, his manner like that of a small and frightened creature. He notices the writer watching and glares back at him, ruefully, pitifully. The writer steals a short drink (a liqueur?) from a deserted table beside him, and swallows it in one go, shudders, and leans back in his chair, head against the wall. At this moment, the writer is unable to leave himself. The actor is unable to leave the role of the writer. They cannot wander into the lives of those other people. Each is trapped inside his role, that of ennui, or work. Life is quickening past them. The writer would feel better, surely, if he were walking on a street at night and happened to glance inside one of those windows with a light on inside. Curtains closed a quarter of the way on either side. Seeing any of these people alone in that room might help him to see them as they are and not as they themselves would like to be seen and in doing this he might forget himself: in seeing them live he might remember that he too lives, and remember how that feels. He has not read, nor heard what happens after this scene, whether the writer does kill himself, or if he finds something in life to live for. The character might even do as suggested, and find the light of a window to wash himself in, and see anew how another lives, and thus find some reason to continue to do the same. He likes to think the character does, but he is sure he does not; rarely does a life end well, especially when it belongs to a character in a film. Now that this is written, it is difficult to know if the current writer is recounting people that have been seen as he sat outside the cafe in his describing this scene, or remembering the video; or whether some people are from his memories of the video, and others from the street of the cafe are combined in this memory. He is not even sure if it matters.

8.

When he used to watch freely, before he knew he himself was watched (recorded), he saw many things he should not have seen. And this particular scene vibrates with a quiet insistency. There was a window in an old complex of buildings, a complex that had the air of a castle, complete with a square in its centre. He used to walk through the complex at night—winding through its entrances and exits, past the folds of closed curtains, and shut blinds—unseen, as he had thought. There was one window on the ground level that was hidden by two squat old trees, unless one stood between their trunks. From here he first saw a man, about eighty—wearing a dark-green jumper over a collared shirt, with lank white hair combed to the side—dead in his armchair. The man's eyes had remained open, looking, until that last moment, out at the leaves and branches of the trees that brushed against his window and did not stop. He slipped in between those tree trunks, more often than he would have liked to admit, to match this dead gaze, to search it for something he could not understand, until one day the body was gone. Soon the trees were trimmed and a family with a multitude of young children moved in. From what he could see, nobody would be alone in that small flat for a long time. He removed that window from his nightly itinerary, but often thought of those dead eyes. It was not guilt that brought them before his mind's eye, but guilt accompanied them each time, floating around the edge of his thoughts. It seemed wrong to leave the body of a person alone without notifying the authorities. Illegal, even.

9.

Soon after the beginning of the landlord's intrusions, and a few weeks after his mugging, his boss called him in for a chat. (These events seem to be toppling over each other. The more memorable moments, those times when "something happened," often something undesirable it seems, are very clear, but the intervening periods are mostly irretrievable: islands surrounded by rising water. It will be said that this chat with his boss occurred a month or two after the mugging. And really, it is impossible to be sure when the landlord began to enter without knocking, all that can be known is that the landlord had not always been so invasive with his presence.) His boss told him he was under investigation for some matter that she could not discuss with him until the investigation was complete. He was free to continue working or take garden leave—his decision would not affect his pay which would continue for the foreseeable future. She smiled, and paused. She said she could not say anymore, but would be happy if he wanted to ask any questions, just not while he was in her office, and not to any of his colleagues. She suggested he ask his questions somewhere where he would not bother anyone else. On her screen he saw a website selling golfing equipment. She had selected an electronic buggy.

He sat at his desk for a while, then turned off his computer and left. He could sense his colleagues watching him, turning to continue after he had passed. Even this building had cameras, he realised, as the security guard did not nod like he usually did when he passed through the security barriers. He stared at the guard. How long had he been watching from that booth? Did his boss have access to the cameras, too? Or had the police notified her about her possibly deviant employee? She hadn't said who was investigating him. He didn't ask. He was afraid.

He stirs a wooden spatula in the pot, lifting it and watching the thick red sauce drip from the end before lowering it back inside the pot. The woman from the museum chops green vegetables beside him. She is methodical, her wrist see-sawing over the chopping board. Now she leans toward him—the knife held at her waist—lifts his hand, and licks the end of the spatula. He says something. She nods, puts down the knife, and carefully lifts the board and empties the pale choppings into the pot. He resumes stirring. She pours more wine into her glass. They wear matching aprons. Behind them, in the dark living room just beyond the open kitchen door, the gleaming figure of a naked statue can be seen, its muscular back turned to them.

He only returned to work a few times since that meeting. He had been sleeping in later and later, and found it difficult to wake early enough to leave his apartment so as to arrive at a respectable time. When he did go back, there was nothing for him to do. Everything he had been working on had been shunted elsewhere. He asked around, but nobody seemed to remember anything different. He noticed a spreadsheet from one of his previous projects on the screen of the guy who was sitting next to him (a person he hadn't seen before): "When were you given that," he asked. The guy took out an earphone and said: "Hmm? This? Feels like I've been grappling with it all my life!" "Yes," he said, "but who was working on it before you?" "I couldn't be sure, mate," he said, then turned back to his computer, and replaced his earphone.

He stopped leaving the apartment. He made excuses: it was too cold; too hot; too windy; the weather might turn. He didn't need milk, nor bread. He would promise himself to get it the next day, then sit at the computer, looking at funny pictures on the internet that were not funny, reading irritating comments. The internet was no place to seek help, not for someone like him. The answers were probably very close but barred to him, and it is tempting here to make the comparison to the windows of the streets and the windows of the internet browser: both accessible, and access to both watched by unseeing and devious eyes. He tried to console himself with the fact that he was being paid. He hid when he heard the front door open. He crept under the bed, and closed his eyes until the man left. There was still some rice in the back of the press, and some mackerel in a tin. The supermarket was full of cameras.

Every shop has one of those dark upside-down domes in a corner, usually more than one. A fly's eyes, separated and stuck to the ceilings (flies secrete a glue, that's how they stick to walls and other impossible surfaces). These he found despicable. They hide their gaze, unlike those more honest cameras that point like a finger toward their target. These blackened domes see in every direction. They are an evolved species. Malicious. And he immediately searched for them the second he entered a shop. He checked the corners of the ceiling, and when he saw them he panicked, realising he had given his self away. No other person is aware of these. They cannot be looked at directly. In that moment his gaze raced to something else, a bottle of wine; or worse, the eyes of the security guard, who had probably already been alerted to his challenging gaze by the one who watches everything the camera sees. They followed him. Between the shelves, his back sweating, he wants to shout that he is innocent, but there is no way to communicate this to security. Innocent him stumbles and if anyone talks to him he will stutter and they will see guilt in him, it will reach out to them as a starving person reaches out to passersby in the street. They will tease his guilt from him. He looks only at that which can be bought. Waits in line. Buys anything. Only criminals go into shops without wanting to buy something. Nobody goes into a shop and walks out with nothing. He is a customer and nothing else, he thinks, the only other option is to become a criminal and he is already too close to that. Oh, to have been able to watch somebody! To have become a statue again, to have lost that self in the beautiful and spare existence of one who is alone! A dignified loss, not like this.

Three severed heads in discussion at the kitchen table. One female, and two male, resting on three plates with a cup in front of each one. The female tries to drink from her cup; the rim is too high. The others stop speaking and watch her attempts. They stick out their tongues, stretching them as far as possible in her direction. One curls his tongue, while the other's remains flat (and shortened). She does the same (her tongue stretches flat) and licks the side of her cup.

10.

He lost sleep. He woke, certain a black dome had emerged from the ceiling and hung there stolid and watching him. He would pretend to sleep, and listen to hear its very slight whine as it angled itself for the clearest shot of his head. He would wake throughout the night believing this, and only when he had fully woken would he check and be certain he had dreamt it, or check to be certain it had not escaped from his dream, and he would sleep for another hour before waking again and suspecting again. Sleep gradually became something he remembered, a pleasant and welcoming country he had once been to.

He stopped going to the museum at lunchtime; it was no longer his lunchtime: he was free to eat at any time. No, it was the woman who had stopped. He no longer saw her, despite forcing his self to travel into the city on the train (a camera in every carriage) solely to see her in those first few days. The tease of the trains' sideways gaze, the back gardens, the bedroom windows! And the camera at the top of the carriage staring, waiting for him to look just that second too long—he would close his eyes and remember past scenes until the train had reached the station. He never had a plan for what he would do when he met her, or he did, but this was more of a building desperation. Maybe talk to her. He had nobody to talk to at that time, apart from the landlord, and he was not prepared for that. Without her the statues became colder. They would not miss him. He would miss them, and the woman, and why had they never spoken? He agonised over this. She would understand his concerns. Are cameras male or female, or does it depend on the gender of the operator? Does the lens dilate when excited?

A tiny cupboard of a room, about six paces in length. Yellowing wallpaper peels in places. "Three old chairs,

rather rickety; a painted table in the corner on which lay
a few manuscripts and books; the dust that lay thick upon
them showed that they had been long untouched. A big
clumsy sofa occupied almost the whole of one wall and
half the floor space of the room; it was once covered with
chintz, but was now in rags." A young male, what can be
seen of his beard is sparse and brown. He is lying on the
sofa. An overcoat barely covers his restless body. He turns
to the left, to the right, throws out his arms and buries
them beneath the coat again. "His head on one little pillow, under which he had heaped up all the linen he had,
clean and dirty, by way of a bolster."

11.

He would change. The idea came quickly: he had mistaken
another man for his self in the reflection of a shop window on a
street one night and, watching that man, noticed he had a limp
like that thug who had robbed him, which made him look down
at his legs to be sure that he hadn't been limping, to be sure of
his self, sure he wasn't remembering, transposing the memory
of witnessing that mugging on the police station's screens onto
the street in front of him. He hadn't. He wasn't. But he could
change. He would alter his behaviour when in public to the
extent that the cameras would imagine they were recording him
but they would only see an act, the puppet whose strings were
pulled by him from deep inside his skin. The cameras would
still see him, of course, but what they see would be a projection
of something that was not him, the way a chameleon takes on
the colour of its background, while retaining its own colour for
whenever—what exact colour they are when themselves is not
known, but it is hoped that there is a time and place when they
can be their true colour, for their sake. But to become someone
else he first had to know himself, and what did he know of his
self, apart from his likes and dislikes, his history, his watching:
each one was a feature of his interior. He might as well have been

living in a building the outside of which he had never seen, while proclaiming that, yes, of course he knows what it looks like; who would live in a place so long without knowing something so elemental. He bought a spy camera, waterproof and quite cheap, and placed this outside the kitchen window; he would watch his self. The idea to change was partly inspired by his reading of a Sherlock Holmes story. Holmes had disguised himself as an elderly bookseller who invited himself into Watson's study, moments after Watson had bumped into this character in the street outside:

> "Well, sir, if it isn't too great a liberty, I am a neighbour of yours, for you'll find my little bookshop at the corner of Church Street, and very happy to see you, I am sure. Maybe you collect yourself, sir. Here's *British Birds*, and *Catullus*, and *The Holy War*—a bargain, every one of them. With five volumes you could just fill that gap on that second shelf. It looks untidy, does it not, sir?"
>
> I moved my head to look at the cabinet behind me. When I turned again, Sherlock Holmes was standing smiling at me across my study table. I rose to my feet, stared at him for some seconds in utter amazement, and then it appears that I must have fainted for the first and the last time in my life. Certainly a gray mist swirled before my eyes, and when it cleared I found my collar-ends undone and the tingling after-taste of brandy upon my lips. Holmes was bending over my chair, his flask in his hand.

This was Holmes' first appearance since his apparent death in the Reichenbach Falls. He had come back from the dead, from the abyss, the gray mist of which now swirls before Watson's eyes, blinding him from reality. He wanted to become not Holmes, but the mist itself. Something to blind the cameras. The way Holmes becomes himself again, it is almost irritating the showy nature of it. What was Conan Doyle thinking when he gave Holmes that easy arrogance? By then, he was apparently tired of his creation; he had attempted to kill it, but was forced, by the fervour of his thousands of readers, to resurrect the character. Holmes had become immortal despite his author's wishes, lived on past his creator. (This situation is not exactly alien to that of the current writer's.) He was sure that if asked how he felt about this immortality, Holmes would say something like he deserved to live, that he was a man of science, unlike his creator who had given up science to dabble in the imagination—forgetting, as people like him do, that for a character, to be born is an act of imagination.

12.

He sits in the armchair with a book in his lap looking through the window at the camera he has installed in the alley. He falls asleep watching a film. He picks his nose. He sits very still, with his profile toward the camera, and remains like this for half an hour, seeming to depart from the room so that his body becomes a piece of the furniture, a prop body made of papier-mâché.

Watching the recordings of his self he did not feel that ownership, or tenderness, that one necessarily feels toward one's self. It is impossible to tan or burn the skin when the sun's rays are mediated by the glass of a window. Not everything gets through the glass, yet it feels like it should. The heat is intense, but the skin does not prickle or take on that smell that is the result of the sun unlocking something that until then had lain dormant in the skin. It is possible that by watching his self—through the mediation of a camera—on that screen, many of those aspects that make a person a person were removed, so that he only saw the shell of himself. Because through that screen he did not really care for what he saw. It was him, but not him.

The landlord sits at the kitchen table of his tenant's small apartment, typing on his tenant's laptop. He types slowly, for two hours.

An email arrived in his inbox. "Don't worry about the windows
. . ." There was a link. He didn't recognise the address. He
ignored the message but whenever he checked his email—and
he did this very frequently—he hovered over that link. About a
week later, it must have been, he replied asking who the sender
was, and who did they think he was that he would click on a link
from someone he didn't know. A message came back immediately: the mailer daemon insisting that the address did not exist.
It was irritating, but not too surprising, that somebody knew
about his needs. How could someone not know, considering the
constant surveillance he was under; they were probably already
investigating his deviancy. He saw how those cameras looked at
him. He finally clicked the link. It was an app that connected
you to whatever CCTV systems currently operated within the
area.

A few days later, his phone dropped through his letter box.
He suspects it did, because he found it on the doormat one
morning. Circumstances were folding themselves around him.
What could he do, reader? Isn't this what always happens? things
occur and occur and soon you are not where you thought you
had been. Almost everyone is conveyed through life. The phone
was packed in one of those bubbled envelopes. Sent from the
police station: they had caught his mugger, and were delighted to
be able to return his phone to him, but his wallet was regattably
[sic] unrecoverable, the note said. It was written in a scrawl, the
signature unreadable. He thought of ringing the station, and
planned to do so the next day, but gradually the urge to ring
faded, and he was happy to have his phone back, excited about
the app waiting in his email. That's too strong a word, he was
interested in trying it out. That's not true. He felt that he had no
other option but to download it, that this was ordained. Or that
they knew what he would do, they knew him more than he knew
himself, and this was just one of the many things that they knew.

But still he persisted in pretending he didn't understand what
was happening. He pretended that circumstances were not lead-
ing him by the hand. Surely it was better not to do anything and
try to live like everyone else, who so obviously knew that cameras

saw everything that happened outside the home but did not care. It was fine to be recorded your whole life, to be captured in fragments that could be knitted together at any moment, whenever anyone says a word against you. Why was this something only he seemed to worry about? This worried him, his worrying about something apparently so normal was worrying. He could have resigned himself to the cameras, let them see what such things see, and his life would have been little different to that of everyone else; he was wrong. This was ordained.

The app wasn't free. But he was on paid leave and it proved to be easy to use: he managed to get it working by the time he got off the train. Without his trying, it displayed the perspective of the camera closest. The train station interior. Crowds flowed from the train and roamed through the hall, their pattern reminiscent of dirty water draining from a bath. He was among them, hidden from the camera among them; until he found himself, a piece of dirt washed free, swirling, his head bent watching his self. He tracked his movements as he walked to the museum on what must have been one of his last attempts to catch her. Or it was his last visit to the office. Wherever it was he went, he remembered the feeling of it being an ultimate visit.

The landlord enters, rolls up his sleeves, and roams through his tenant's rooms, picking up objects, examining them, writing what must have been notes in a little pad he takes from his shirt pocket. Through the open kitchen door, he can be seen in the bedroom, flinging the sheets off the bed, and leaning over the mattress, as if checking for a body.

He often thought about bringing the recordings of his landlord's intrusions to the police. On the first day they had met, the landlord had told him that he had been a sergeant in the police but had taken early retirement. "Men like me have links that go deeper than anything you know," the landlord had said, tapping his nose. "You'd want to watch yourself, sonny, especially in the position you're in." Those notes the landlord took might have been for the police, for the investigation, he thought. If he had brought them to the authorities, it would probably have speeded the progress of the investigation. If something is inevitable, why not bring it closer in time and be done with it, rather than letting it hang in the future, waiting for your arrival, for you to walk beneath it. He had always treated deadlines as things that might disappear if ignored; few are so kind. And really he would have preferred to end it then.

He took to leaving the apartment just so he could watch his self on his phone. In the streets, he watched, via the CCTV cameras, the way he walked, how he stopped, the strange jerk of his neck when he turned to follow a sudden sound on a seemingly empty street. The edges of the screen were an ugly substitute for the frames of the windows. Being a romantic, the tall windows of the city's larger homes, with their thickly painted frames, were among his favourites. Elegantly slim curtains cinched at the waist, broadening at the bust and hem on either side of the window: his favourites. Then there were the barely framed windows seen from below, minimal with edges of dark silver, a television on the wall, a man tending to a bird, the fluttering wings of which can be glimpsed inside the curved edge of its cage. The asymmetrical, the bay, the tilt and turn, sliders and the casement; a lace curtain lapping at the wind through a raised sash window. The screen of his phone could not match the breadth of the city's frames, the wonders they held, so unconscious, and present. And his self, there, hunched inside that black plastic of his phone, surrounded by it.

That stranger on his screen in the darkening light. It was so difficult to place this person who strode past the shuttered shop windows with the living stuttering person he had believed his self to be. This was someone who couldn't possibly share his essential nature. Watching his self he experienced a sensation akin to looking in the mirror and seeing the reflection scratch its earlobe while one's own hands remain in one's pockets. He was so tired. Yet he, the vision of his self onscreen, did not look as tired as he, the watcher, felt. It was clear that one of them was wrong.

The landlord leaves yellow legal notes on clothes, shoes.

Wear this today, wear this in two days' time, they read. There are notes on the fridge indicating what food he should buy. The landlord does not seem to write these. He pulls them from a plastic bag, and places them around the apartment with a weary automaticity.

These notes greeted him when he arrived home after watching his self on the streets. He did not obey them. They were trying to break him completely, and he would not. They could wear him down to his skin, bury him in the ground among the past, but he would not acquiesce. (And he didn't, not really.)

Increasingly, his spy camera that peered through the kitchen window recorded the impossible. It was as if his apartment had taken on the duality between the person he knew himself to be and the energetic, more confident person he saw on his phone. It did, he thought. Everything was dividing. If he was honest, he knew he increasingly went out to return and find what had been recorded in his kitchen: to let the spy camera record his absence, to let him see a world without him. It seemed the recording would reveal something new each time he came home. He wasn't sure if he could only see these scenes through the mediation of the camera's lens because it recorded that which did not exist or because it recorded things that he could not accept, things that had occurred, but which he did not allow his self to see, to believe.

He is cooking his dinner and wearing a shirt of the sort favoured by the landlord, a pinstripe with a large white collar, though the sleeves are rolled to his elbows. He is bald like the landlord, too. He walks through the apartment the way he does, checking, typing, taking notes. He shakes his head often. He makes tea and watches the television—his bald head blocking the screen.

13.

He would return from watching himself in the city's parks and streets, and find visual evidence of his having been in the kitchen: evidence for his having existed in two places. Via his little camera, he was confronted with this other, external memory of him, and it appeared so much more reliable than his own memory that he had no option but to accept it, to live with the idea that he was no longer one person but two.

> The wind cries and whips. The skin of someone is between the lens of the spy camera and the glass of the kitchen window, only the skin is too granular and its patterns too shifting to be something as fixed as skin; it is much more alive than skin: a sandstorm blowing through the kitchen, but it is clear that this is neither a person nor a kitchen but a desert, but there *is* a person there, on the left of the screen, arm raised against his forehead, leaning forward, climbing wearily through the sand.

He recognises his self on the screen. The camera follows him for hours, yet he was asleep when this was taken: the timestamp runs from midnight to four in the morning, following his journey through the sandstorm. He watches all four hours of it.

One shouldn't exist anymore, soon he will not exist, and this seemingly new person will. A plant that is poorly suited to its environment will die. Sometimes, a parasitic seed will attach itself to this plant, to its stem, and draw all of the nutrients to itself. When this occurs, everything beyond this attachment will wither, while this new branch will grow strong and take over until there is nothing left of the original plant but the stem below the initial attachment. Otherwise, it is a completely new plant.

14.

Passing the museum, where he used to spend so much of his time, his head turned downward, facing the screen of his phone (out of habit, mostly), the screen switched to a CCTV feed from inside the museum's entrance hall.

He is walking through the vast white space, nodding confidently to the two guards who sit on chairs on either side of the room. Something is said, and all three laugh. There is an object in his hands, but it is difficult to be sure what it is. A rifle? He continues out of shot, then another clearly shows him enter the Hall of Sculpture, and the woman is there! and he walks right up to her! He reveals a bunch of flowers from behind his back and they hug. A lingering kiss. He poses beside a statue, like a tourist, and she takes a photo before he bursts out laughing. She joins him and together they leave.

He had been standing outside the museum entrance since he had seen his self enter it, and now he realised he would have to hide. From behind a De Chirico display in the gift-shop window, he watched as his self and the woman, their clothes and skin a welcome combination of navy, cream, and beige, walked onto the street outside. It was beginning to rain. The scene bore a similarity to one from his past which briefly overcame him (best friend, a girl he fancied, betrayal, lust, tears).

Returning from the past, he missed which direction the woman and his self had taken. Knowing a little of his self, he guessed they would head back toward the centre of the city and so ran in that direction. His phone's screen showed the streets, always just ahead of him. Finally, in a crowd on the main street, he saw them. They were walking close together, along a street parallel to the one he now stood on. He walked slowly, following, watching. And they were speaking very seriously; each held the entirety of the other's attention. He felt a little pride at that, knowing he had set the foundation for this relationship. They paused at a shop window. She pointed at something that could not be seen from the perspective of the CCTV, and he nodded. They turned back and entered a restaurant, one he would never have gone into. As he glanced at the entrance, he realised his other self had been dressed better than his own self. His other self's clothes were fitted, and more pleasing to look at. It was clear that that was not really him, but the shell of him, his skin, bones, his body and clothes because he was still here on the other side of the screen, so whatever that was in there, that man on the screen who had strolled inside that restaurant, that was not him but a projection of him, the promise of him. A person of the exterior. The person he had created to act as a screen to hide from the electronic eyes of the city. Really, he should have known this would happen. It was his fault for not anticipating this.

Someone cleared their throat behind him, and his first instinct was to stare harder at the screen. It was a policeman with his hands tucked into either side of his armoured vest. "Are you all right, there?" he asked. "Fine, thanks," he said, and put the phone in his pocket, and walked back onto the main street before he could say anything else. They'd have footage of him skulking into the alley, he thought, probably why the policeman followed. (Had he recognised that face? Those hands?) And footage of him leaving too. A fine little interlude for the final cut, the resolution of the investigation into his activities. Looking back he saw the policeman watching, and muttering into his radio. A camera positioned on the side of the restaurant seemed to point at him. This was one of the more obvious ones, its intention undisguised. He was almost grateful for the honesty of these earlier models.

15.

This other man who shared his appearance, did he also share his memories? Had this other version of himself only come into being since he had begun trying so hard to be normal, or had he always been inside him, a secret? He should have spoken to her before, on all those afternoons in the museum, he knew this now, but he had felt somehow that they had both wanted this silence, that they had a greater bond through silence than they could ever have with words. There had been an eroticism in their lack of talk, in their touch, a companionship.

He visits the museum at lunchtime in the hope of seeing the woman again. The statues have gone, temporarily, a sign says, and in their place is a new exhibition. Cameras, small ones, are placed all over the walls, leering, and in the centre of the room, a group of large, giant cameras, standing up to eight feet tall, are clustered, facing outward in a defensive posture. In a darkened room to the side, a wall of screens displays what it is the cameras see. He sits in that small room and watches for a long time. It becomes clear that this is an archive of what the cameras have seen rather than a direct transmittance of their vision. He forgets himself.

> People examine the cameras, and sit in the small chairs in the corners of the room to contemplate the meaning of the exhibition. This is a place where one is allowed to stare. At one stage he sees her, but she is with him, his other self. They stroll through the room. They are drinking from takeaway coffee cups, large cups that require both hands to avoid spilling.

The other self had been living with him without his knowing it. He noticed one day another door beside the bathroom. It was half the width of a normal door and it was locked but he kept an eye on it as he drank tea at the table. After some hours, the other came out, and went into the bathroom. The spy camera outside stopped recording around this time. He didn't bother fixing it. Neither did he. He had seen enough of what happened in his kitchen, too much of it. The landlord continued to enter with his key. They hung out, the landlord and his other self, drinking in the kitchen, playing cards, inviting friends around while he, the dwindling self, stayed in his bedroom, reading, trying to read, seething, because this was exactly what he had wanted, to have someone live for him while he barely existed, so he could watch without interruption. This had been his dream. Strangers would open the door to his room and stare incredulously. He would explain that they are twins, he and the other. Many of the strangers called him the evil twin, asked if his name was Hugo, and why he wasn't locked away in the attic. They were mostly drunk when they said this, or high on something, and always seemingly about to spill with laughter. He only rarely explained the apartment's essential lack of an attic, or that if he were the evil twin he would not be named Hugo. Most of the time it cannot have been a mistake to open his door. The bathroom door swings open when the handle is not securely turned and nobody does that unless they want to lock it. And the apartment is not that big. They must speak about him, he thought. In there, at his table, they laugh at him. He couldn't find the key to lock his bedroom door. It is impossible to relax in a situation like this. Sometimes, without saying anything he would leave the apartment by the front door, and sneak around the side, to the alley, where he would watch them in his kitchen. What he was looking for he was not sure. Often he woke in the alley early the next day, shivering.

16.

His bedroom door narrowed to half its size, while his other self's door increased by a half to become a full door. He noticed this one day as he returned, sneezing and sniffling, from the alley; there was nothing to indicate that this transformation had been recent either. The plaster, the frame, the wood, everything appeared to be as it had always been except his door was now halved. He confronted his other self about this soon after. The other self almost seemed afraid of him; he even promised he would speak to the landlord about it. He did not want that, but he did not want his other self to know he did not want that so he said nothing, and went back to his room.

The statues from the museum have crowded the kitchen. One leans on the counter, in front of the microwave, the curly hair of its head in its hands. Another, Venus (fully armed), just covers her naked body with the open door of the fridge. The figure of a man sits at the table, carving a blade; his blind eyes look up and to the side. A small child, Cupid, perhaps, points at the camera. A gargoyle climbs the larder; the arch of its bent back, one claw, and the tail are visible, the rest obscured by an open press. He is in the alley in front of and to the side of the camera. It is raining and he is staring inside at his other self whose face can be seen in those of the statues. (He sees himself in each one, and they are melting because they are not the original statues but plaster casts.) He has picked up a rock and is crashing it against the glass of the kitchen window.

The woman from the museum took to visiting the other self. He knew this because he watched the CCTV near the apartment from his bedroom. At first, his other self kept her from him, probably jealous of their perfect relationship before his arrival, he thought. Of course, he watched them from the alley, imagining how it would be if that were him in there, imagining what he and her would talk about, how much they would have in common. It is possible there would be nothing between them, he thought, and they would no longer feel that frisson if they were to again see each other in the museum. They would smile at each other as if they were old work colleagues, just a short smile.

He met her when she visited one evening. His other self was out. The other self had begun to leave more frequently, spending most of his time away from him. It was clear the other self felt disgusted by his old and sad self. He invited her in, and pretended he was the other. This barely worked. In the short time the other self had lived, it had experienced more of life than he, it seemed, and much of it with her. He couldn't keep up the pretence, yet he suspected his other self's not being in the apartment when she arrived was not a surprise to her. She said she knew who he was. She said it with a smirk.

She was eager to talk. She said she had followed him. It wasn't a confession, but more of an invitation to finally discuss their shared silences. The way she said it, there was an expectation that they had followed each other, that their games had extended beyond the confines of the museum. She had watched him as he had sat alone in the kitchen. She had stood in the alleyway for hours (almost exactly where the camera had recorded from), the two of them less than ten feet apart, her believing they were immersed in this communication that had so suited them, he alone and lonely. He admitted he had never followed her, but she didn't believe it: "Stop pretending," she said, "you're being very strange, of course you followed me, I heard you, felt your body against me on the bus, felt your gaze as I ate my dinner; the men's footprints in my flowerbed, the trail of soil from there to the road outside, of course you followed me, stop denying it." He had been sure before her outburst, but perhaps he had followed her, and had forgotten, but, no, he couldn't believe that. He was not so broken as to believe that. He then wished he had followed her before, so that they could have arrived at this point without the insidious mediation of his other self. When that self did not return home, she said it was getting late, and she had better go.

17.

He followed her.

She wore a jacket, skirt, and pumps. Bare legs. Cameras whined as they turned to follow him. Before them, he crept naked in his deviancy. She walked slowly. He followed, his runners scuffing the ground every few minutes as he glanced at, and away from, the cameras. It had been a while since he had last left the apartment, and it seemed there were even more cameras than he had remembered. If only his glances were physical, could harm, destroy that electronic gaze, free him from it. He watched the roll of her hips, and her arms, the rhythm between the left and the right, the way her hair swung in perpetual catch-up to her limbs. Was anyone still watching, or was this footage to be reviewed in the morning: the night-stalker at play. How her skirt tightened and released. Would they watch her, too, or was she not part of the investigation? This wasn't right. He should have mentioned the investigation, let her know the extent of his deviancy. He was not just a museum-goer. He was not fully with her, not lost, but conscious, overly so, despite their closeness, conscious of her awareness of him, of the camera's unceasing gaze that filled the space between them, rendering it impersonal and alien to him, and yet he still felt some of the thrill of continuing where they had stopped so many months ago in the museum, but now that he was aware of the cameras, he felt uncomfortable. The urge to speed up and overtake her was too strong. What was the cause of this urge? To allay her probable fear? To allay his projected feelings of her fear? Or was it to display to the cameras that he was a decent sort, the type of man who seeks to spare the feelings of people when they are vulnerable, the type that should not be investigated. Was this urge to do what is considered right not a part of his other self? (He had assumed the other had taken with him all those urges toward normality and conformity, leaving him individual and quivering, and that this was the cause of his increasing delicacy.) Or was, he wondered, his wanting to speed up to walk with her an attempt to deny the other competing urge that lurked deeper inside, an urge belonging to that primordial part of him that existed only for sex, food, rest? That part of him that had, at times, continued to watch at lighted windows when he shouldn't have? That part of him that went beyond certain thresholds? To her, to the cameras, to himself, he was less a voyeur than a predator, stalking this young woman through the dark streets of the city. Shop windows were lit and filled with headless mannequins, some naked, others clothed. Strange uncomfortable postures. But she must have known it was him she heard behind her. Her stride was unbroken by those emotions that overwhelm the body in moments like this. There was no panic in her slim legs, no hesitation in her steps. Her knowing made it worse. It made him realise his feelings were not for her but for himself, his sense of morality, or worse than that, it wasn't even for him or his moral principles, but it was for the cameras themselves. There was a deep guilt inside him and knowing its possible source only made it worse. He was an uroboros of guilt slithering through the silent streets.

They were passing by the centre of the city, through streets that feel so different when empty, so melancholy or newly born depending on his mood, on the time of day. She tripped on a broken tile, and fell forward, arms stretched to lessen her fall. For a moment he considered turning and racing home, waiting for his other self to arrive so he could tell him she had fallen. Let him help her. After a few seconds he rushed to help her, relieved to reveal his self to her, and to show the cameras that she knew they were playing, that he was not wholly the actions they saw. They walked the rest of the way to her apartment together, her arm around his shoulder, his around her waist. "It's such a pity I fell," she said, "I felt a real thrill knowing you were there: my silent mirror." He assented, not wanting to appear foolish for having worried. Because he was worried, he was worried he was dreaming, or he was worried because this did not feel like the daydreams where he had pictured such a meeting between them.

18.

When they had reached her home, and he had helped wipe the grit from her bloodied knee, he asked why she had stopped going to the museum. She said she had been away on work in a different country. He was relieved to find it wasn't because of him. She joked about the museums she had visited, that they had been boring without him to stalk her through their rooms. The use of that word felt wrong. In fact, she seemed wrong. They were sitting on her small couch, gazing at each other, their thighs pressing. She stroked his cheek: "You are so serious," she said. He stood up, and said he had better be going. She flustered: "Wait a minute, I wanted to show you something. Do you want to see me, really see me the way we used to see those statues?" Now he felt flustered, yes, of course he wanted to see her, of course, but his other self . . . were the two of them not going out? could he cheat on . . . his self? It wasn't possible.

She took his stillness for a yes, and walked toward a closed door. "Look at me," she said, and opened the door, "eat me up with your eyes!" There she was inside the room, a complete likeness of her, sitting on the bed, holding an empty mug in her lap, shoulders slumped forward, hair tied in a bun, while the woman who was still smiling had her hair down, sleek and bouncing when she strode through the streets. It wasn't a statue, but a mannequin, exactly like her. Even her makeup, the subtle lipstick, the black that traced beneath her eyes, though the clothes were different. This one was dressed more subtly, the colours of her clothes more muted.

Not knowing what to say, or think, he said: "That's you," and immediately felt like an idiot for stating something so obvious. "Yes, it is, and this is what I look like when I am alone—look." With a strange eagerness, she roughly took the mug from its hands, and placing the mug on the side table, pulled the hands to its forehead, as if she were tortured by a headache. She looked up at him: "Try it, put me in *any* position you like," she said. The presence of this mannequin sitting so forlornly with this too-cheerful woman standing beside it, this woman telling him to manipulate its position, changed the atmosphere from one of flirtation to something that went beyond perversity. He felt sick. "Go on, try me," she said, her eyes sparkling.

The eyes of the mannequin focused on his. Dark-brown eyes. He saw her face now, saw the life that was unmistakable. He saw what he had always searched for, and here it was in a woman alive and pretending to be dead, no, not dead but something that never lived but seeks to emulate the living. She had become a statue. He knew then that this was the woman whom he had known in the museum, this is why it felt so strange to follow the other woman—she had been the wrong one, the other self of the woman he had known. And still, he wanted to pretend he didn't understand, he wanted to manipulate that woman's body into the poses of the statues, make her into all of the people he had ever seen alone, place her before the window each time and go outside and watch her through the glass. See her. But he couldn't. "Are you okay?" he finally asked. She glanced at him, her eyes amused. She unfolded herself, stood up, fixed her skirt, and walked out of the room and toward the front door. The other woman ran and blocked her way: "You can't leave, she can't leave—she's under investigation," she said to him. He said he was, too, glad to be able to finally admit it. "Yes, but she hasn't been afforded the same allowances as you." This surprised him; he had assumed the investigation centred on him was private, that it was only known by the authorities, the police, security guards, the unseen viewers of the cameras; but now that she also knew, he wondered why he had ever believed it would be private. Why wouldn't everyone know? She might give him information. "How do you know?" he asked, "what is the point of these investigations?" "You want to know too much," she said. "If you were being investigated for something that was being kept from your understanding, you would want to know too!" he said.

"No, I mean that you are the focus of an investigation because you want to know too much, you're too greedy, always searching for things that don't belong to you, wanting to dig inside people's lives, wanting to see them the way they are instead of the way they would like to be seen. The fact that you can't understand why you would be investigated speaks to the very need for you to be investigated. Your behaviour is intolerable, just like hers. You're just like her!" She turned to the other, the woman, the one he had known, had loved (did love), who had been standing observing the conversation. The woman from the museum smiled at him, and he heard her voice for the first time. "Were you sent the app, too?" she asked. Hearing her voice was slightly anti-climactic, being as it was the same as the woman's whom he had been speaking to all night. Still, he appreciated it, and convinced himself that her voice was of a better quality than that belonging to her other self. "Yes," he said. She linked his arm, and said, "Shall we go?" while at the same time she pushed her other self away from the door. He felt sorry for the other and was about to suggest that she was better suited to his other self anyway, when she spat on the floor after them. Fine, he thought, that's fine.

The cameras watched as they walked. "You know, most statues don't last very long; that's why the museums create casts of their figures. People steal the statues, and sell them on to expensive hotels, and private collectors, drug dealers, and billionaires," she said. "Oh, I know," he said, and told her about the kitchen recordings from his spy camera, the casts of the statues melting.

Two small and separate spots of light appear, both against marble, each in different parts of the darkness. Both hesitate over aspects of the marble; one is now focused on the muscular strain of a thigh narrowing to a bended knee, while across the room the other illuminates a face, the nose, and heavy brow creating shadows, holes in the light. The white brow is wrinkled and soft human fingers massage what might have been worry or thought. Now the hand is lower, stroking the robe, the fingers exploring the folds of the stone fabric. On the other side of the darkness the other hand can be seen to caress and rest over pale toes. It is as if the two holding the lights were trying to communicate with the marble, collecting each of its secrets with their fingers. The lights carefully follow the hands as both trace the living lines of the figures, collecting images until an observer could bring them together to form two frozen figures that just as they are fully seen begin to recede into the dark piece by piece as the lights draw together.

The room is suddenly lit. Black-clad figures race from the doors and converge on the man and the woman, who cry out, but this cannot be heard. The man and the woman reach for each other. Their arms are grabbed by the others who surround each one, and secure each of their hands together, and carry the two from the room. The room is empty again. The statues remain, lost in their eternal search. The lights are turned off. It is imagined that a sympathetic observer might still see these small flashes of light tracing the lines of those statues, but these would only be afterimages, visual memories of the scene briefly imprinted on the eyes and falling away until there is nothing.

19.

They were released a few days later. He was kept in a cell that
was not particularly large or small, but the smell was unbearable.
When he complained of this, he was moved to another cell,
which was fine, apart from the window that was too high to see
out of. A camera in each corner of the ceiling. His meals were
delivered through a hatch in the door that slid open several times
a day. Mostly a pair of eyes were seen—rarely the same pair—
gazing in at him as he sat on his bed. The hatch must have been
well oiled because he never heard it open; sometimes he would
glance up, and catch them staring, and the hatch would slide
shut. On leaving, they each received a brown envelope. Little
was said to them. There were no restrictions on their behaviour,
or admonishments about their past deeds. In fact, all he knows
of their crime is what her other self told him, and now that he
knows of their essential duplicity, he does not believe what she
said. There must be some other reasoning, but no one he asked
told him, not the police, the jailers, the judge who judged him
in some distant courtroom while he sat on his thin prison bed
picturing scenes from books and films in lieu of real people,
patching together what he could remember of his past, those
aspects that might create some understanding for him, for her,
for anyone who reads this. He assumes he and she do not deserve
to know why they were punished, that to tell them would be to
reverse their punishment which is the erasing of their identity.

Inside the envelopes were invitations to their funerals, which
noted that they were not obliged to attend, and neither were they
to inflict bodily death upon their selves just because they were
being pronounced dead. If they were happy to attend, the invitation continued, it is necessary that the dead wear appropriate
funereal wear. This was followed by a website link and phone
number of a local mortuary and a formal-wear rental shop. At
the bottom of the page was a phone number for a volunteer-run
helpline, with an addendum that this service would not be available to them after their funerals. Stuck on the end of each letter
was a small and round yellow sticker: a sad face.

It was particularly kind of the authorities to release them together, he thought. They went back to his apartment, but his landlord had changed the locks. When they knocked on the door and rang the doorbell, his other self refused to let them in. He opened the door when they knocked but when he saw his old self, well, he didn't see him, if that makes sense. He looked past him—not pretending, just not seeing—and closed the door again. They tried her place, but they were just as invisible to her other self, though he is sure he saw some recognition in that other's eyes. They found themselves on the streets, and the streets overflowed with windows.

He watched his coffin disappear behind a black curtain and into an unseen furnace. A lot of people came: his co-workers, family members he had not spoken to for years, his landlord. At least twenty people, more than he had expected. He was given no particular role or place to sit. Many cried throughout the ceremony, and it was touching to see people who were strangers united, if momentarily, by their mourning. Nobody spoke to him. It was the idea of him that they mourned, the projection of him that belonged entirely to them, which really had nothing to do with him as he sat there. What, he wondered, did they feel about his other self, that newer living one; was that someone they welcomed? Stupid question. Of course they did. It was safe to mourn him because death sat in that room and he was it. The dead, as it was written, shall have no dominion. They have been grieved for—he and she saw this—in the church and the funeral parlour, from outside the pubs where he and she spent the rest of the day following each funeral. It was real, and not just put on for the benefit of the newly dead, because they do not exist for those people. Before he and she are fully gone, he would like to visit all of those people he had once known. Wait outside their homes, and finally see them as they are. Incidentally, he has seen his landlord alone, in his apartment. He drinks, heavily. When he is not refilling his glass, or pouring it down his throat he could almost be a statue. He has watched him many nights and each time this is what he sees (five heart attacks, indeed!). There were far more attendees at her funeral, as he had expected—but he was not jealous. He is not sure if he was allowed to be at hers, but nobody stopped him, nobody did anything to him. The current writer supposes it doesn't really matter what people like him and her do because they are dead, effectively. They signed the documents—produced after the razing of the empty coffins. Legally dead: they have no claim to the living, not even the personal pronoun, hence the distance from the person that is written about here: the dead are not allowed to take part in life, not even in words.

The authorities have taken their things, including their names, because these must be retained for the living. He and she are nameless like those statues whose dates are guessed in little plaques in the museum. Their bodies: representations of the people they once were. Figures etched in time. The others, as the careful reader will have noticed, continue to live among his and her possessions. He and she possess nothing, they barely have each other. Their gaze is the gaze of the dead as life runs past it in the public spaces. The dead love the parks in the daytime, and at night, the flat complexes, the grand old roads with their large homes on the edges of the city, the suburbs with their multitudes: finding those scenes framed by so many different windows, watching for the moment another comes undone. In these moments, it is easy to forgive them, all of them. These two figures barely break the stream of passersby in the narrow paths of the city. Soon their bodies will join them in death; that is unfortunately a consequence of how they must live, outside of life, but for now, they have been given that which they have desired. They have become the gaze.

On the left, a man wearing a white silk shirt, sleeves buttoned at the wrist, sits on the edge of a comfortable, pale-pink armchair, reading a newspaper, the top of which he leans on a round coffee table in front of him. There is something else on the table, something flat, maybe a magazine or placemat. The walls are painted the colour of parchment. Above him are two framed paintings, though the one on the far left is obscured by the black window frame. The one directly above her appears to be a city scene, maybe that of a park behind which tall buildings can be seen. On the right sits a woman on what might be a piano stool, in a red dress with a ruffle or bow barely visible on her right shoulder. Her body faces us, but her gaze is on the piano's keys, or something propped above them— it is hard to see where her attention lies because her face is mostly in shadow. One finger is placed on a white key, though she has not pressed down in what feels like a lifetime, but could only be a few minutes. Time means little now. There is another framed painting above her, a darker one, or it is the shadow cast by the light that darkens it, a shadow that divides her side of the room from his, so that he, on the left, is in the light, reading the news of the day, while she—on the right, in the darkness, one finger on the white of a piano key—might be anywhere.

On the Absence of Light

1.

WHEN THE WORLD FIRST BEGAN to turn from the sun, pulling that new light until it broke against a fallen leaf, or the cap of a mountain, which, from the perspective of the sun, must have looked like a pebble, it created infinitesimally small absences of light. The world turned and the absences grew, spearing and then cloaking deserts, forests, fresh oceans; and the world pulled the darkness around it.

2.

Amerighi da Caravaggio painted his studio black. Pinholes in the ceiling let the light peer through. He is there, face emerging from the shadows, holding a lantern obscured by the helmet of the soldiers arresting Christ. He watches us through the tired eyes inside Goliath's severed head; he emerges from the vast darkness to witness the murder of St. Matthew. Bellori, his first biographer, believed "Caravaggio's stylistic habits corresponded to his physiognomy and appearance. He had a dark complexion and dark eyes, black hair and eyebrows, and this, naturally, was reflected in his paintings."

3.

Remember, we could not speak the language, and the bus stopped, and the driver motioned for us to get off on that rutted road that smelled of roasted manure. After a while, a town shimmered up from the horizon, slowly creating itself in readiness of us travellers. We measured the earth's imperceptible turning by the length of our shadows drawn before us as we walked. And now those same shadows reach across the clutter of my desk. I turn on the lamp and my own vague image jumps, darkly, against the wall behind me.

4.

When Christopher Marlowe and William Shakespeare wrote their way to immortality, the title for those people who would act out their words was shadow. You were a shadow on the stage and a man on the ground. When Macbeth was first told of his destiny, in a 1933 production of *Macbeth*, directed by Theodore Komisarjevsky, his ghost was portrayed by a shadow. Henry Irving used man, shadow, and light to portray the ghost in different attempts to produce that perfect play: a silhouette in 1877, a trick chair in which the shadow playing Macbeth was seated in 1887, and a shaft of light in 1895. It is fitting that Irving dithered between his representations of the ghost, not knowing whether it was man, or shadow, or light, when these shadows are identified as Plato's flickering images projected onto the cave wall.

5.

On the tennis court we were each multiplied by four. You fell, and the crack echoed through the winter night. Your selves coalesced as you lay on the ground. The doctor showed us the shadow of your delicately named bones, your tibia, your fibula; she showed us the cracks that looked like hairs had stuck to the

image. I wouldn't be writing this if I hadn't wanted to brush
them away.

6.

There are three constituents of a shadow: umbra, penumbra,
antumbra. I hold my hand between the lamp and the desk's surface. The darkest place, where my hand blocks the direct rays of
electric light, is the umbra, Latin for "shadow." The penumbra
(almost, nearly shadow) is the partial occlusion of light, where
the darkness is less severe, seen in this case, emanating briefly
from the edges of the umbra, from my dark finger tips. The
antumbra is something that cannot be described.

7.

When Odysseus moored at Oceanus, he dug a hole for an animal sacrifice to summon Tiresias of Thebes. In Hesiod, Erebus
is the god of darkness, born of Chaos, father to Charon, the
ferryman. Homer gives this name, Erebus, to the underworld.
Shades soared up from the recently dug pit. (Odysseus drew his
sword to guard the animals' spilt blood from their thirsty dead
mouths.) The first to arrive was Elpenor, his old companion.
They sat in gloomy conversation: "I, on one side, holding out
my sword above the blood, and on the other side, the shade of
my companion speaking out." The shades, the umbras, the places
most absent of light. It was only recently that we relegated shadows to a phenomenon known only by the occlusion of something more substantial. Where light cannot reach, there will be
shadows: cheap toys for poor children, barely remembered tools
for astronomers.

8.

To say someone is afraid of their own shadow is to say they are
a coward. The shadow waits at the end of the road; why not be
afraid of that ultimate destiny. E. A. Poe has a character describe
the voice of a recently deceased friend whose speech rings out to
haunt his own wake: "The tones in the voice of the shadow were
not the tones of any one being, but of a multitude of beings,
and, varying in their cadences from syllable to syllable fell duskly
upon our ears in the well-remembered and familiar accents of
many thousand departed friends." *Are You Afraid of the Dark?*
Do you remember it? The teenagers, our forever elders, sitting
around the campfire telling horror stories. It must have taken
all your strength to hide your fear: I never saw you raise your
hand to hide behind, never heard you yelp at the reveals, even
during the episode when a girl's face was stolen, and beneath we
saw an absence of features, smooth skin, a tiny puckered mouth.

9.

The Mayans were wrong, Nostradamus has not yet been proven
right, but men of science extrapolate—this is different to proph-
esying, so different the two barely share the same letters—that
the sun's brightness will increase steadily each year. In about 7.7
billion years, it will expand through the remains of our ozone
layer, past our closest defences, and take us in its fiery arms
until we become a burning light, and future historians will say
the earth died by celestial cremation. Caravaggio created his
life as if it was another painting, but it was more a myth than
a life, and he was not a god. On the run from Rome, he disappeared. "Thus was Caravaggio reduced to leaving his life and
bones on a deserted beach" (Bellori). The shadow of death is on
every face. There are numerous theories as to Marlowe's death,
many involving arguments over money. Queen Elizabeth and Sir
Walter Raleigh feature in some of the more interesting accounts.
In any event, he died in 1593. Shakespeare died many deaths, as

is fitting. Theodore Komisarjevsky died in San Remo in 1905, the same year in which Henry Irving died, hours after performing as Becket. Macbeth, having been fooled by the Witches' prophesies, delivered in turn by armoured head, bloody child, and a crowned child carrying a tree, died at the hands of Macduff. Unfortunately, Plato had no Plato to record his death. He died in his bed in 347 BC, accompanied only by a Thracian girl, who serenaded him with a double-reed flute. "The girl could not find the beat of the *nomos*. With a movement of his finger, Plato indicated to her the Measure" (Vogelin [whose last word, incidentally, before he himself died, was Plato]). Plato died in tune. Like Macbeth, Odysessus also sought knowledge of his destiny from the shadow world. After speaking with the shade of his former companion, the shade of his mother arrived, then came Tiresias, one-time advisor to Cadmus, robbed by Athena of the sights of the present and gifted with the sight of the future. He prophesied the death of Odysseus would come from the sea. Telegonus, born of a brief affair between Circe and Odysseus, had been sent by his mother to find his father but was forced, by dangerous weather, to land on Ithaca. Not knowing this to be the home of Odysseus, he set about stealing cattle. Odysseus challenged his unknown son. In the ensuing fight, Telegonus, not recognising Odysseus, killed his father with a spear tipped with a stingray's poison. Poe was found lying unconscious on a plank outside a pub in the autumn of 1849. He died in hospital after four days of suffering delusions and comas. The last words of Giacomo Leopardi were a request for the window to be opened so that he might see the sun. He died in the arms of a friend in Naples, in the summer of 1837. If this piece of writing is to last, and I will be expending a sufficient amount of effort to insure it does, then I cannot say I am the only one of this illustrious circle—into which I shoulder aside a place for myself like some Dunning–Kruger test case—who is not dead. I may be dead when the, always, dear reader gets around to reading this, say when they find it taped inside multiple waterproof envelopes hidden beneath what used to be my floorboards, or stumble upon this ancient blog of mine on what will be the old internet.

Or I may be still living when the reader buys my house at an inflated price and decides to install tiles and uproot the pine. Thus, for the purposes of the dear reader, I am both dead and alive, darkness and light, in other words, a shadow, like you. And yet, I know there is more to me, that my shadow is still bound to the souls of my feet, striding behind me in the mornings, rising up to meet me in the evenings. I still enjoy the heat of the sun, the lustre of the moon, the brightness of the long-lasting light bulb. I wonder if they will have affordable Oakley sunglasses in the future, with built in X-ray vision. I wonder if you, the you who knows who you are, the you who is not the dear reader, but you, I wonder if you will come back to my life, or will I ever meet you again. Somewhere. Later. (If I were dead I would know this, but I am only hypothetically dead, and that is apparently not enough.) Do you remember when this rhyme was just a game, and not a tired reference to the plague, not a tired reference to life. I think it is best understood when sung by children, or chanted by passionate, underground cults. Ring-a-ring o' roses, a pocket full of posies, a-tishoo! a-tishoo!

We all fall down.

10.

In the dim light of his father's library, Leopardi wrote of every kind of light, of every shadow, every darkness; I can rely on him, not my possibly dead, probably not, self, to provide these last lines, to communicate that which I cannot: "Most pleasing and full of feeling is the light seen in cities, where it is slashed by shadows, where darkness contrasts in many places with light, where in many parts the light little by little grows less . . ."

(Within This Space)

THE DOORS CANNOT BE LOCKED anymore, and yet the artists are rarely seen outside of their rooms. They are afraid to leave, mostly. Sitting on their bed or at their desk, looking out on to the gardens, filled with broken statues and overgrown trees, that roll out toward the horizon, the gardens that open onto the mountains and into the sky, they cannot create. It is only when they leave their rooms that they hear my words. These words linger in the air of those long corridors, in the surrounds of the great communal rooms, in the other artists. Many have reported a sensation similar to waking from a dream only to find it fall away when they return to their rooms too late. There is a delicate line that must be travelled between that small and comfortable living space, and that wider, estranged space that is the greater part of this building.

It is thought that this is why they stay in their rooms: they cannot bear to lose themselves, their ideas, their art, which they think of as a part of themselves, though few say this out loud—they find this loss so difficult that many choose not to hear me. They would prefer to live dully, safely rather than experience that uncertainty. This may be why those who do roam never stray too far. And when they do, they realise, often too late, that their wandering had been a mistake, that they are forgetting. (It is a given that nobody wants to hear about those who remain in their rooms, those who remember but do not create, not even those who choose to do so would like that—especially not those; no, it is always more exciting to dwell on the aberrant, the small details that sway the eye from otherwise perfection, the human.) Many of the artists have been here for longer than they can remember being anywhere else. Most have forgotten that there could be an anywhere else. Most, but not all. It would be very boring if it were all.

They often disappear. Where they go is a mystery to them, as the entrance is rarely there when artists want to leave, when they try to leave, when they walk those long corridors in despair at their seeming inability to leave, despite their having walked through the large front doors quite easily on that very first occasion. Doors, naturally the most agile of a building's inner structures, tend to become walls, and so forth, they say.

Now and then there are artistic events. When outside of their rooms, they hear voices, or a singular voice, or rather they intuit when and where this will occur: I speak differently to each one. (Usually the event is held in the conservatory, or the ballroom— although this latter location has become inaccessible ever since an artist's skin suddenly enveloped him, suffocating him, and continued to grow so that it can now be seen bulging from those grand double doors and narrow stretched windows. In the winter months events are held in the library.) It would be rude to discuss this, so everyone trusts that everyone else receives the same warm message, and nobody asks. These events are almost the only time in which every artist begins to think about travelling so far from their room. To do so, they might enter into a collective consciousness: a waking dream weaved from each one's imagination, or the dregs of dreams that idle when the artist is said to be living.

On hearing me say this, an artist gasped as an idea arrived just as she opened her door, and is now busy creating, on the clean white walls of her room, a map of idle dreams. And now she races from her room in search of markers of an immediately necessary colour (for that strange terrain, I assume). By the corridor's fifth turn she has forgotten what she is running toward. She returns to her room and is bewildered by the scribbles that run from the walls to her thoughts—shadows of something she can no longer understand. She resolves never to leave her room again.

She starves. They are so fragile, they could blow away with the draft from a distantly closing door, some say.

H has been here for what feels like a year, though it may be more, or less, but he likes to think of it as a year. His neighbour is young. She told H she is a painter. She has been here so long she has forgotten her name; that is not unusual, everyone has forgotten their name, but she has even forgotten that people are supposed to have one. During their conversations over dinner, when H (for the seemingly last time) tells her that everyone should have a name, she invariably says, "I see, but not artists, surely?" or something of that sort, as if artists were other. Monsters, animals, deep-sea creatures, beasts, and instruments through which myths are played. And she might be correct, but most doubt it. They have had this conversation so many times, and always at this point she looks off, away from him, at nothing it seems, or at a point that is inside her thoughts, which her eyes can only indicate, and politely excuses herself. The more cinematically inclined refer to this as the Bergman look. Though H has forgotten his name, he has not forgotten the importance of the convention, that it provides a verbal anchor for the person, for others to call, to roll on their tongue with love, to throw in anger, and more importantly, it is the crown of one's identity, something given and which one grows so close to one feels bereft in having to give it up: an occasion that rarely occurs inside a life, it must be said. Usually the name is all that's left. H cannot think why he forgot his name. Though he does not know what this might mean, the flurries of understanding that arrive now and then—always out of reach—worry him.

I suspect it might return if he left this space. He hears me and soon begins to suspect this too. This suspicion lingers in the dark of his thoughts for a few days, then blooms, and he feels he must find his name (it is not really H, nor does it begin with that obnoxious rugby-post). H accepts that this is something he must do. He puts it down on his list of obsessions (an artistic trait, apparently, and not at all an affectation) and goes about finding the entrance so he can find that anchor of his self. He brings a notepad and pen to pin it down inside its own letters.

They will be so jealous—H will be the first artist to exist here with a name, he thinks. He will enjoy especially their envy, but also the triumph of, yes, an identity. Being here, they tend to lose themselves, even those who stay cooped up in their rooms.

The name is usually the first to go, and then the characteristics, the individualities; or rather, it is those that have been otherwise formed through living among others that go, leaving behind the self, the quivering core of a self. This is most frightening for those who have no self, it is like paring down a jelly to find there is nothing at the centre, only they cease to be there to discover this unfortunate, and ultimate, fact.

Somewhere along the way from his room to the conservatory is where H thinks he entered this building. Incidentally, just here, behind one of these doors, an artist has left the window open. A grim and ancient raven has flown in and waits for her to return. It perches on a porcelain cast of a skull—sectioned and labelled according to the beliefs of phrenology—and practices its lines. The raven will have to wait a while longer; she is spending the night in the room of another artist. They rarely hear me when in their rooms, though I hear everything they say, and think; I hear their essence wherever they are, their being. Even with the door closed, a luminiferous ether can be seen to waft from beneath it through to the corridor where H walks. The raven cries.

He is too busy thinking to hear that erudite bird. About halfway down this elegant corridor, which he frequently passes through, there is a wide set of stairs which he is certain he climbed in that first walk through the building. The stairs had continued upward for hours, opening onto large landings which only led to the next flight. He had fallen against the bannisters with dizziness so often, with so many steps, turning and turning to climb again and again, and though he now feels they were surely insurmountable, he must have continued, otherwise, he reasons, he would still be outside, living in a different way, perhaps not even as an artist. Now H follows the stairs down. With each proceeding floor they narrow and finally open onto a wide, unpainted corridor, a sort of basement, or what used to be the domain of waiters, cleaners, kitchen staff, etc., he guessed (in fact these labels are not his, he saw only flashes of uniform, snippets of memories of such staff from things he has read and watched, embellished by his sensitive and artistic nature so that they resemble nothing that might ever have existed). He walks through a spider web. Something drips far off: rain water, the saliva of a guttural. A gutter. He follows the sound, in search of the outside.

He wakes up in his bed with the memory of an underground tunnel found in one of those unmarked rooms he had walked by in a corridor down there. It opened from the floor, as if someone, or some creature, had torn a way up from the earth. The tunnel split in two after a few metres. He chose the left tunnel and continued another couple of metres where he found a new choice of two. Rather than risk another decision, he turned back and tried the other tunnel, the one on the right. Again this split into two. He is not sure if he remembers this or thought of it just now. He hears me say this and he becomes sure: yes, he remembers. He looks out the window. The trees bend in a strong wind. The head tumbles from an old statue. It is raining, but in this room he hears nothing; the rain loses most of its power, it is almost invisible, and now, forgotten. In his room the idea of the underground tunnels becomes incoherent, the possibility of the tunnels becomes a distant statement that runs ahead of him into that system of strange tunnels, so that he only sees glimpses as it turns each corner of his thoughts, always just ahead of him. He doesn't mind. They might only have been the memory of a film he once saw. A film filled with underground creatures, blind things that of course preyed on those vulnerable humans who ventured down inside the old earth. The cold earth, I mean.

This building, this immense and baroque space filled with sumptuous, frigid decor, is thought to have been the favoured summer retreat of a long-dead European dictator. H thinks it must be Franco. Others suggest it was a dictator of a country which is only now European. Nobody really knows where this building was built. It might even be in America, but none of the artists appears American, not South, Central, or North, so

nobody entertains that idea for very long. One artist is convinced that this dictator and his family take turns living through
her. At the moment, she believes she is the dictator's little dog.
Her immediate neighbours find her all-night barking quite bear-
able compared to her attempts to steal their belongings, and to
persecute them for being the wrong sort of artists. They find it
most worrying when other artists line the corridor and salute her
as she passes. They make notes of this and of course forget the
reasoning behind those angry sentences, those deep indentations
and broken pencils.

Over dinner—they are eating in the oak-panelled dining
room—a rare occasion—H asks his neighbour whether she can
remember the way she came in. She is not sure. She might have
been born here, she says, or maybe it was just yesterday that
she wandered in from the street. Neither is sure of anything so
far from their rooms. The distance induces a giddiness. A large
man with red cheeks and little hair and more years behind him
than is fair yells, "Food fight!" and flings his trifle at the diner in
front of him—a young, sullen-looking boy. Handsome men and
beautiful women giggle and launch plates of steak and halibut in
the air. H's neighbour pours her wine glass over his head. There
is a freedom so far from their rooms. They play, but it is lacking
the seriousness with which children play. It is tiring, violent in
its frivolousness. The artists usually fall asleep before they can
return, slumped in the corridors like something out of Brueghel
(the elder). Sometimes they forget themselves completely and,
from the windows, can be seen to be lying in the garden of statues. Of course they cannot return, and often they have even forgotten that they might want to, and so they die there—the grass
quickly covering their artistic poses—I will not say how many.

Watch this artist pause and pat his pockets for a pencil to
write with. He has heard me. A collage of food is now balancing
in the forefront of his mind. The food of each socioeconomic
class, at times replaced with archetypical personas from that
class—possibly a collage of a food fight. And yes, inequality will
figure, he discovers as he rushes to his room. The idea will not
make it. I didn't like it, anyway, and hopefully he wouldn't have,

either, otherwise he would be a poor artist. He could even be a fake—I detest those. Taste is everything. Burn the pretenders. Yes, I don't like him. He hears this and tries to twist it into some kind of art, but it is really just sadness. Still, there are some who will enjoy it.

Now and then a conspiratorial huddle can be found to block a corridor. They are almost impossible to dislodge, packed tight, usually in between the marble columns that jut from the walls. Other artists get stuck, and these are invariably far from their rooms, and so on the verge of delirium, and the obstruction becomes greater until a decision is made, or one pulls the others into a nearby room which almost always belongs to one of the group. At times, such is the force with which they push and argue, they merge with each other, arms stuck inside backs, fists in faces. Luckily there are only three in this present grouping. They are on their favourite topic: "Perhaps all artists are guilty of something," a tall lady says. "No, no, it is not that we are guilty, no court could ever decide that, no, we are *presumed* guilty," says an equally tall male. They enjoy being able to meet each other's eyes without having to stoop. They smile at each other, smiles wholly unrelated to the conversation. A shorter artist taps the lady on her arm, "I think he's right, do you think we have been locked up in here for the crime of being artists?" Without breaking her gaze from her tall companion she says, "Uh-huh, that's, yeah, that's probably it." The taller male suggests they retire to his room to further the discussion. He has spotted a perpetually saddened neighbour, one who aims to make art from the future, or by it, coming up behind them, and is anxious to condense this little grouping rather than expand it. He opens the door to his room, which is just beside them, and ushers the lady inside. The much shorter artist manages to squeeze himself through the closing door. The futurist wanders past, glancing absently at the empty picture frames that seem to grow on the corridor's walls. He sees each one before he sees it with his eyes—such is the nature of prophets. He sees the Persian carpet wrinkled by their hasty footsteps, and neatly, sadly, skips over the danger.

Nobody knows when all those large gilt-laden frames were

emptied of their paintings. Nobody knows where those paintings are. They are buried in a deep grave twelve miles from the south-ernmost wall of this building. They are barely recognisable. There is an artist there, too. He thought it would be clever (something to do with the process of mummification, I remember). And it might be, in the future, when he and his painted shroud are eventually found.

H wants to find his name. I want to believe it is more than the usual artistic obsession, but I do not think there can be any-thing more than that, especially in an artist. H is still waiting for his work. There are many who never produce, who live in anticipation, the waiting; oh, how they wait. They will catch an idea, as if by accident, as if it had stuck to their hand like some splattered insect, and carefully examine it until a flaw is found: the flaw that will allow them to release it back into the building. They seem to misunderstand the function of the artist's role. Unfortunate beings—or perhaps these are the clever ones, the ones who say they are too good for art, those who have seen the dangers of art, the ones who will not make that sacrifice. The others surround these individuals at times, questioning them about what they might make. This pressure might explain the many disappearances, but some who have disappeared were supposedly accomplished beings. H calls the missing artists by another name, he says they are the escapees. They have found a way out and decided they do not want to return. H is also in love with his neighbour. She, the painter, may be in love with him.

An elderly artist has just now been speaking to H. He has also sought out the entrance he says. "You have to tell me, where is it?" H says. "You misunderstand me, I have never found it," the old artist adjusts his cravat, tightening then loosening it with his finger so that his neck can crane without constraint. "I was never an artist to begin with, you know, I came in here looking for someone, a girl; her family told me she was staying here. I thought they were lying, and they might have been, they were bad folk, now that I think of them, but I had the day off and it was nice weather for a walk. Well, after a bit of bother at the entrance, I finally got in and asked the bellhop by the stairs where I might find her. He said she was probably in the dining room considering the time, and sent me down a corridor without any doors. Or maybe there were doors but they were locked. Or it was a gravel path between statues, fine ivory ones. On my way back I met someone else who sent me off in another direction. He was wearing a beret; must have been the first beret I had ever seen aside from the films! After what felt like hours, but, no yes, I am sure it was hours, I wanted to go home, I had begun to think she wasn't there, you see, or she was but I was forgetting about her, but nobody I asked seemed to know anything. I thought they were on drugs, but I know better now. I ended up staying the night in the one room with an open door. There was a window that looked out on a garden full of broken and fallen statues, and here I am. In the same room as that first night, I think. There are less heads on the statues, now. I still look for the entrance, you know, but I suppose I do it more out of habit than anything." "It must be calming to go looking for it," H said, thinking about his own grandad and how he used to enjoy his walks around the neighbourhood.

"The building changes, it flexes and it bends, even the plants in those giant pots, they move, they do, I've seen them crawling down the corridors at night, a trail of dirt behind them. They want out as much as we do. It creaks something awful at times, I hear this and think, ah, now there's someone looking for a way out. It knows us, it does, better than our mothers." H decided not to tell him about the tunnels in the basement, and wished him goodnight. "Did you not want to join me?" the elderly artist asked. H shook his head: "I really should get back." Close by, a bicycle bell rang out. A younger man came cycling past them, asking directions for the way to the sea. Both ignored him; while this building might appear to be never-ending, it surely cannot contain the sea, they thought (they should think less), then they watched as he slowed before a particularly sharp corner, ranting about building a canoe, it seemed. He won't build anything, he won't see the ocean. He has hope, and that's all he has. He hears me say this, but doesn't believe it. He has probably heard my parenthesised aside, and this is what gives him hope.

There are books everywhere, but the majority can be found in the library. Lovely leather- and (what is said to be) skin-bound books, and of course paperback ones, too. All of them are empty, not even the spines have any words printed on them. Not even a hint of ink. Lovely. No one to say I wrote that, that's mine, or at least it was, or ask the most loaded question: And what did you think of it? Be honest now. Hmm. The artists like to hold these as they sit in their rooms, sleeping after a heavy dinner. They rest port bottles on the empty books. Lean them against their pillows. There are writers here but none has written a book like these. Those writers marvel at the blank pages, saying quietly among themselves, how brave to leave it like that, how many words might have ruined this book, how many words were unwritten from these pages. How pristine! Those artists could never resist like that. Look, there are two artists examining the clean pages of a book just now. A fine new one. They are standing in the threshold of a room. They are barely visible so white are their clothes, skin, and hair. Ethereal, one might say. Another artist wants to see, but they keep angling the pages and standing so that the two of them fill the threshold leaving the third artist in the corridor, unable to see anything but the leather cover. All three are neighbours, but factions continually form between them. Today the artist in the corridor, the one wearing tortoise-shell glasses, has found herself by herself. Nobody talks through-out this serious pantomime, but there is tension winding in this third artist; suddenly she shoves the book out of their hands and shouts, "You will find nothing in those pages, anyway, I don't know why you look at them so often!" and runs off to her room, slamming the door behind her.

Just a little along the corridor is an artist collecting an armpit of books that had fallen across the floor. He has been here too long, he thinks. So long he has no memory of his childhood, and so he has a fear that he will become something other than him if he does not remember. He has a point. He hears me say this and nods vigorously in agreement. You'll find it in the books, I say. (He'll never find it.) He pretends not to hear this definitive statement. You'll never find it, I shout. Ha-ha-ha. My voice echoes through his bones. His face is red, the colour of indignation, of blood, of life, I guess. In fact, many artists think there is something in their childhood that will show them, I don't know, the truth? themselves? It is a pity, really, they try and try to find something that has been extinguished, reaching back into the embers of their past to burn themselves on the flames that once flared. The more intuitive ones know this, and still they cannot help but try, until, until. An ominous word that: until, until what, who?

The elderly artist is wearing a different cravat when he sur-prises H, who is just leaving his room. "Enjoying your walk?" H asks. "Yes, it's a good day for it, a fine day," the artist says. "I meant to ask you the other evening, did you ever find the girl you were looking for? That time you first came here, I mean," H says. "No, never," the artist says, and turns to walk away. "Do you still look for her, like you do the entrance, is that your art?" H calls after him. The artist spins around, his eyes bulging. "Don't talk such nonsense," he splutters. "How am I to live without her, look at me, look, this is my art!" He twists his cravat so that it seems to choke him. H feels overwhelmingly sympathetic toward the elderly artist, but stands helplessly by his door, knowing that he is now the audience, and it would be unethical to interrupt the performance, no matter how anxious it makes him, that this anxiety is surely part of the art. The old man pulls at the ends of the cravat, his face purpling as he chokes himself, and crumples to the floor, his head slamming against a large flow-erpot holding a green fern. It is possible that this is not really the elderly artist's art, but an act of desperation. H doesn't hear me say this, instead he has heard my thoughts, from which he has found an idea for a piece—brilliant, he thinks, amazing, it pushes the idea of his name from his mind. This is to be his life's work, art that is not art, negation that disguises itself as creation—but the elderly artist is lying by the threshold of H's door, blocking H from opening it. Not wanting to disturb the poor man's body that had become an artefact—whether the artist meant it or not, against his wishes, perhaps—but still desperate to commit his idea to paper, H does not know what to do. He knocks on his neighbour's door. The painter opens it and, blinking slowly, asks H what he wants. Unable to find any useful words, H points to what was now the body. His neighbour stands very still and, looking from H to the body and back again, her eyes widening, says, "I'm sorry, I've just the most wonderful idea," and begins closing the door before pausing: "What am I thinking—I'm sorry, so sorry, did you know him?" "No, well yes, a little, we spoke just a few days ago, or maybe it was last year," H says. "I see, well that might work, too," she says as she slowly closes the door, leaving H the only one breathing in the hall. Her behaviour annoys him, naturally, but also adds to his growing excitement, everything now seems connected, it all flows toward what he will do, if only he could write it down. Already the ideas, the images are losing their shape, becoming soft, and yielding, giving way to thoughts of dinner—how thirsty he just now realised he feels. That elderly artist said something about the building shifting, that it is not exactly a building, but a something living. H hears me, and now remembers, thinking that the man had said the building alters its architecture depending on the thoughts and moods of its inhabitants. H closes his eyes and pictures the body of the elderly artist lying in another corridor, far from his room; he imagines he is trying to escape and the door to his room is the door to the outside, that place he barely remembers. H opens his eyes. Nothing has changed.

Acknowledgments

These will be brief. Thank you to John O'Brien for putting his faith in my writing by publishing this collection. Thank you to Susan Tomaselli for publishing many of these stories in the excellent journal *gorse*; for suggesting I put this collection together, and being its first reader. Thank you to my sister, Sarah, for her constant support, and being the first reader of the majority of these stories, at least until the PhD got in the way. Thank you to my mom, Carmel, for gifting me with a love of literature from a young age; but, more importantly, without her I wouldn't be here.

Selected Dalkey Archive Paperbacks

Michal Ajvaz, *Empty Streets*
   Journey to the South
   The Golden Age
   The Other City
David Albahari, *Gotz & Meyer*
   Learning Cyrillic
Pierre Albert-Birot, *The First Book of Grabinoulor*
Svetlana Alexievich, *Voices from Chernobyl*
Felipe Alfau, *Chromos*
   Locos
João Almino, *Enigmas of Spring*
   Free City
   The Book of Emotions
Ivan Ângelo, *The Celebration*
David Antin, *Talking*
Djuna Barnes, *Ladies Almanack*
   Ryder
John Barth, *The End of the Road*
   The Floating Opera
   The Tidewater Tales
Donald Barthelme, *Paradise*
   The King
Svetislav Basara, *Chinese Letter*
   Fata Morgana
   The Mongolian Travel Guide
Andrej Blatnik, *Law of Desire*
   You Do Understand
Patrick Bolshauser, *Rapids*
Louis Paul Boon, *Chapel Road*
   My Little War
   Summer in Termuren
Roger Boylan, *Killoyle*
Ignacio de Loyola Brandão, *And Still the Earth*
   Anonymous Celebrity
   The Good-Bye Angel
Sébastien Brebel, *Francis Bacon's Armchair*
Christine Brooke-Rose, *Amalgamemnon*
Brigid Brophy, *In Transit*
   Prancing Novelist: In Praise of Ronald Firbank
Gerald L. Bruns, *Modern Poetry and the Idea of Language*
Lasha Bugadze, *The Literature Express*
Dror Burstein, *Kin*
Michel Butor, *Mobile*
Julieta Campos, *The Fear of Losing Eurydice*
Anne Carson, *Eros the Bittersweet*
Camilo José Cela, *Family of Pascual Duarte*
Louis-Ferdinand Céline, *Castle to Castle*
Hugo Charteris, *The Tide Is Right*
Luis Chitarroni, *The No Variations*
Jack Cox, *Dodge Rose*
Ralph Cusack, *Cadenza*
Stanley Crawford, *Log of the S.S. the Mrs. Unguentine*
   Some Instructions to My Wife
Robert Creeley, *Collected Prose*
Nicholas Delbanco, *Sherbrookes*
Rikki Ducornet, *The Complete Butcher's Tales*
William Eastlake, *Castle Keep*
Stanley Elkin, *The Dick Gibson Show*
   The Magic Kingdom
Gustave Flaubert, *Bouvard et Pécuchet*
Jon Fosse, *Melancholy I*
   Melancholy II
   Trilogy
Max Frisch, *I'm Not Stiller*
   Man in the Holocene
Carlos Fuentes, *Christopher Unborn*
   Great Latin American Novel
   Nietzsche on His Balcony
   Terra Nostra
   Where the Air Is Clear
William Gaddis, *J R*
   The Recognitions

William H. Gass, *A Temple of Texts*
   Cartesian Sonata and Other Novellas
   Finding a Form
   Life Sentences
   Reading Rilke
   Tests of Time: Essays
   The Tunnel
   Willie Masters' Lonesome Wife
   World Within the Word
Etienne Gilson, *Forms and Substances in the Arts*
   The Arts of the Beautiful
Douglas Glover, *Bad News of the Heart*
Paulo Emílio Sales Gomes, *P's Three Women*
Juan Goytisolo, *Count Julian*
   Juan the Landless
   Marks of Identity
Alasdair Gray, *Poor Things*
Jack Green, *Fire the Bastards!*
Jiří Gruša, *The Questionnaire*
Mela Hartwig, *Am I a Redundant Human Being?*
John Hawkes, *The Passion Artist*
Dermot Healy, *Fighting with Shadows*
   The Collected Short Stories
Aidan Higgins, *A Bestiary*
   Bornholm Night-Ferry
   Langrishe, Go Down
   Scenes from a Receding Past
Aldous Huxley, *Point Counter Point*
   Those Barren Leaves
   Time Must Have a Stop
Drago Jančar, *The Galley Slave*
   I Saw Her That Night
   The Tree with No Name
Gert Jonke, *Awakening to the Great Sleep War*
   Geometric Regional Novel
   Homage to Czerny
   The Distant Sound
   The System of Vienna
Guillermo Cabrera Infante, *Infante's Inferno*
   Three Trapped Tigers
Jacques Jouet, *Mountain R*
Mieko Kanai, *The Word Book*
Yorum Kaniuk, *Life on Sandpaper*
Ignacy Karpowicz, *Gestures*
Pablo Katchadjian, *What to Do*
Hugh Kenner, *The Counterfeiters*
   Flaubert, Joyce, and Beckett: The Stoic Comedians
   Gnomon
   Joyce's Voices
Danilo Kiš, *A Tomb for Boris Davidovich*
   Garden, Ashes
Pierre Klossowski, *Roberte Ce Soir and The Revocation of the Edict of Nantes*
George Konrád, *The City Builder*
Tadeusz Konwicki, *The Polish Complex*
Elaine Kraf, *The Princess of 72nd Street*
Édouard Levé, *Suicide*
Mario Levi, *Istanbul Was a Fairytale*
Deborah Levy, *Billy & Girl*
José Lezama Lima, *Paradiso*
Osman Lins, *Avalovara*
António Lobo Antunes, *Knowledge of Hell*
   The Splendor of Portugal
Mina Loy, *Stories and Essays of Mina Loy*
Joaquim Maria Machado de Assis, *Collected Stories*
Alf Maclochlainn, *Out of Focus*
Ford Madox Ford, *The March of Literature*
D. Keith Mano, *Take Five*
Micheline Marcom, *A Brief History of Yes*
   The Mirror in the Well
Ben Marcus, *The Age of Wire and String*
Wallace Markfield, *Teitlebaum's Widow*
   To an Early Grave
David Markson, *Reader's Block*
   Wittgenstein's Mistress
Carole Maso, *AVA*

Harry Mathews, *My Life in CIA*
  Singular Pleasures
  The Case of the Persevering Maltese: Collected
  Essays
Herman Melville, *The Confidence-Man: His Masquerade*
Steven Milhauser, *In the Penny Arcade*
  The Barnum Museum
Christine Montalbetti, *American Journal*
  The Origin of Man
  Western
Nicholas Mosley, *Accident*
  Experience and Religion
  Hopeful Monsters
  Imago Bird
  Impossible Object
  Judith
  Metamorphosis
  Natalie Natalia
  Serpent
  The Uses of Slime Mould: Essays of Four Decades
  Time at War
Warren Motte, *OULIPO: A Primer of Potential Literature*
Gerald Murnane, *Barley Patch*
  Inland
Mihkel Mutt, *The Inner Immigrant*
Yves Navarre, *Our Share of Time*
Dorothy Nelson, *In Night's City*
  Tar and Feathers
Boris A. Novak, *The Master of Insomnia: Selected Poems*
Flann O'Brien, *At Swim-Two-Birds*
  At War
  Further Cuttings from Cruiskeen Lawn
  Plays and Teleplays
  The Best of Myles
  The Collected Letters
  The Dalkey Archive
  The Hard Life
  The Poor Mouth
  The Short Fiction of Flann O'Brien
  The Third Policeman
Máirtín Ó Cadhain, *The Key/An Eochair*
Patrik Ouředník, *Case Closed*
  Europeana: A Brief History of the Twentieth Century
  The Opportune Moment, 1855
Arvo Pärt, *Arvo Pärt in Conversation*
Robert Pinget, *The Inquisitory*
Raymond Queneau, *Odile*
  Pierrot Mon Ami
Ann Quin, *Berg*
  Passages
  Tripticks
Ishmael Reed, *Juice!*
  Reckless Eyeballing
  The Free-Lance Pallbearers
  The Last Days of Louisiana Red
  The Terrible Threes
  The Terrible Twos
  Yellow Back Radio Broke-Down
Noëlle Revaz, *With the Animals*
Rainer Maria Rilke, *The Notebooks of Malte Laurids*
  Brigge
Julián Ríos, *Larva: Midsummer Night's Babel*
Augusto Roa Bastos, *I the Supreme*
Alain Robbe-Grillet, *Project for a Revolution in New York*
Daniël Robberechts, *Arriving in Avignon*
  Writing Prague
Olivier Rolin, *Hotel Crystal*
Jacques Roubaud, *Mathematics*
  Some Thing Black
  The Great Fire of London
  The Plurality of Worlds of Lewis
Vedrana Rudan, *Love at Last Sight*
  Night
Stig Sæterbakken, *Don't Leave Me*
  Invisible Hands
  Self-Control

  Siamese
  Through the Night
Lydie Salvayre, *The Company of Ghosts*
Severo Sarduy, *Cobra & Maitreya*
Nathalie Sarraute, *Do You Hear Them?*
  Martereau
  The Planetarium
Arno Schmidt, *Collected Novellas*
  Collected Stories
  Nobodaddy's Children
  Two Novels
Asaf Schurr, *Motti*
Pierre Senges, *Fragments of Lichtenberg*
Elizabeth Sewell, *The Field of Nonsense*
Bernard Share, *Transit*
Youval Shimoni, *A Room*
Viktor Shklovsky, *A Hunt for Optimism*
  A Sentimental Journey: Memoirs 1917-1922
  Bowstring
  Energy of Delusion: A Book on Plot
  Knight's Move
  Life of a Bishop's Assistant
  Literature and Cinematography
  The Hamburg Score
  Theory of Prose
  Third Factory
  Zoo, or Letters Not About Love
Kjersti Skomsvold, *Monsterhuman*
  The Faster I Walk, the Smaller I Am
Josef Skvorecky, *The Engineer of Human Souls*
Gilbert Sorrentino, *Aberration of Starlight*
  Crystal Vision
  Imaginative Qualities of Actual Things
  Mulligan Stew
  Pack of Lies: A Trilogy
  Splendide-Hôtel
  The Sky Changes
Gertrude Stein, *A Novel of Thank You*
  Lucy Church Amiably
  The Making of Americans
Gonçalo M. Tavares, *Jerusalem*
  Joseph Walser's Machine
Lygia Fagundes Telles, *The Girl in the Photograph*
Nikanor Tetralogen, *Assisted Living*
Stefan Themerson, *Hobson's Island*
  Tom Harris
John Toomey, *Huddleston Road*
  Sleepwalker
  Slipping
Jáchym Topol, *Angel Station*
Jean-Philippe Toussaint, *Monsieur*
  Running Away
  Television
  The Bathroom
Dumitru Tsepeneag, *Hotel Europa*
  La Belle Roumaine
  Pigeon Post
  The Bulgarian Truck
  The Necessary Marriage
  Vain Art of the Fugue
  Waiting
Dubravka Ugresic, *Lend Me Your Character*
  Thank You for Not Reading
Tor Ulven, *Replacement*
Mati Unt, *Things in the Night*
Paul Verhaeghen, *Omega Minor*
Boris Vian, *Heartsnatcher*
Nick Wadley, *Man + Dog*
  Man + Table
Markus Werner, *Cold Shoulder*
  Zündel's Exit
Curtis White, *Memories of My Father Watching TV*
Douglas Woolf, *Wall to Wall*
Philip Wylie, *Generation of Vipers*
Marguerite Young, *Miss Macintosh My Darling*
Louis Zukofsky, *Collected Fiction*